Of Laughter & Heartbreak

<u>Books by Angela Grey</u>
Spirit Pass: A Jessica Stone Novella #1
Missing and Murdered Indigenous Women & Girls: A Jessica
Stone Novella #2
The Lasting Echo of Lost Souls: A Jessica Stone Novella #3
Resilience Throughout Recovery
Beyond Quirky
Run Fast, Run Far
Sifting Through a Storied Past
Coteau des Prairies Runaway
Prologue to an Epitaph
A Childhood Lost to the Wind
Secret Whispers
Déjà vu
Beating Drum of a Broken Heart
Nostalgic Tendencies, Idyllic Endeavors & Current
Inclinations
Between Shadows and Lies
Bedridden & Gutted to Mindful
Bdote
Dreamcatcher
The Cartography of First Love
Whimsy and Bliss
Ink & Ivy

<u>Also by Angela Grey & Paige Peterson</u>
Lake of Secrets
Dancing Without Music
Echoes of the Past
Echoes at Midnight
Madness and Mayhem
Long Since Buried
Since You've Been Gone
Some Species of Outsider-ness

Of Laughter & Heartbreak

Angela Grey

To the love of my life, Robert, and our four adult
children,
Paige, Cody, Chase, & Brooke,
children-in-law
Vince and Angel,
and grandsons Luke and Logan
—AG

CONTENTS

1 The Sound of Breaking

"We can't keep doing this for her. It's destroying our family," Liam Matthews, a thirty-seven-year-old upper-middle-class, affectionate dad, says to his wife at the breakfast nook in their kitchen.

"I know. Stop yelling. Stevie will hear you," Morgan, a thirty-five-year-old attractive soccer mom, responds. "Over the summer, I'll take her to a therapist to get some help."

"Why can't she just stop? It was cute at one point, then became quirky; now it's insanity," Dad says

"I think that she has a serious problem that might need ongoing therapy."

"I don't want her spending any time with Piper," Dad says.

"Liam, you can't do that. It will just kill Stevie not to spend time around her younger sister," Morgan says.

"But Piper is eight years old and will learn to think all this crap is normal," Liam spews. "We need to save her from her sister's mental illness."

May 15th, 6:02 am
Basement Bedroom
Dear Journal,

My dad bought me this E-Ink writer tablet for reading documents and textbooks, sketching, journaling, and note-taking. It's supposed to be a paper-like writing experience somewhere between an Etch-A-Sketch and a tablet. He thought if I journaled and sketched that, I'd get over my quirks, as he calls them. Truth be told, quirks seem like something optional and can be stopped, whereas what I do is severe, mandatory, and debilitating.

Anyway, hello, Journal. I'm Stevie Matthews: bat shit crazy, soon to be 16-year-old, and just finishing up 9th grade, where my only friends in the world are Izzy and Nico. We met by default in that our names fell next to each other on the alphabetical seating chart with Isadora Madsen and Nicolas Montgomery. And we all have summer birthdays, July to be precise, each eight days apart. That's good because eight is a good number. I don't know what would've happened if it were another number. Well, I do know that it couldn't be thirteen.

And there is part of my problem that my parents argue about as I write this entry. I'm plagued with what you heard my dad once call quirks. Now I'm mentally ill, and they're thinking about taking my little sister away from me. It's probably best. I don't deserve to have anybody because I'm too weird and crazy.

"Promise me, Morgan, no more giving in to her obsessions and compulsions. There, I said it," Liam admits.

"It's easier said than done," Morgan rebuts. "It takes longer to wait for her to do it than if I just go ahead and do it. There's no arguing or crying, plus it doesn't disturb Piper. If I tell Stevie no, I'm just showing Piper that there's something important about what Stevie needs to do."

"Pffft," Liam utters.

"Shh, now, the girls will be in to have breakfast soon," Morgan hushes.

"Hi, Mom, Dad," long, blonde-haired, blue-eyed, precocious Piper says upon descending the stairs from her upstairs bedroom. "What's for breakfast?"

"Pancakes and sausage, sweetie. Sit down by your dad," Jami says.

"Stevie, time for breakfast," Morgan yells down to the basement. Stevie, who's at the top of the stairs, turns and rushes down to the basement.

"Mother, say it the correct way," Stevie responds.

"Oh, I'm sorry," Morgan says, which garners a dismissive look from Liam. She counters, "Stevie, it's time for breakfast."

"I'll be there in a second," Stevie returns.

When Stevie sits down, her tablet brushes up against her fork and pushes it out of alignment. So she stands up, waits for her mother to fix her fork, then sits down again.

"Dad, are you going to pick up that radon detector for me?" Stevie looks to Liam, who begrudgingly replies with a nod of his head.

"Thank you, Daddy," Stevie crosses that off her list on her tablet.

"Why do you need a radon detector? I thought that you had a radon detector kit that you put in the mail?" Piper wonders.

"That is so smart of you to remember, sweetie," Dad says to Piper.

"I plan on using both," Stevie replies, which results in Liam dropping his fork to his plate and looking at Morgan.

"Do you think two are really necessary?" Morgan asks.

"Mom?" Stevie responds. "Isn't my life worth more than the cost of a radon detector?"

"Stevie, one is enough. I'll get the electronic one from the hardware store, so you don't need to send them in anymore," Liam balks.

"Dad," Stevie cringes and holds a hand to her lungs.

"You're not going to get a lung infection or have trouble breathing, Stevie. Do you know why? Because we don't have any radon seeping into the basement," Liam reassures. "I must get to the office. I'm running late."

"You're two minutes early, Dad. Please wait," Stevie begs.

Liam gives Morgan a seething glare but stands in place repeatedly, looking at his watch and the clock on the wall.

When the antique grandfather clock chimes at the top of the hour, Piper flinches and spills what's left of her milk. Morgan jumps up to get the purple all-purpose cleaner to spray down the table.

"Mom, my body can't handle that toxic spray.

You know that," Stevie says.

Liam stands with his hands on his hips, shaking his head. Morgan drops the towel to the table and brings her hands to her temples, and cries.

"I'm trying, everybody. I'm trying," Morgan bawls.

"I'm sorry I spilled my milk, Mommy," Piper says quietly, which causes Liam to throw his head back, then sigh deeply.

"Piper, it's not your fault. You didn't do anything wrong," Liam kisses his youngest daughter on the head and barrels towards the door.

"Dad?" Stevie yells. "You forgot about me."

Liam pauses at the front door with his hands on the trim. He closes his eyes momentarily, then returns to kiss Stevie on the head as well.

"Mom, can you put deodorant on the list? The correct kind this time, please?" Stevie asks.

"Which is the kind that you want?" Morgan makes a list at the counter. "Aluminum-free?"

"Yes, Mom," Stevie says. "I'm done with my breakfast."

"You didn't eat all your food, Stevie," Morgan counters.

"Mother, please?" Stevie waits for her mother to take the plate and clear the table of Stevie's dish, silverware, glassware, and placemat.

Stevie stands up and goes to the half-bath just off the kitchen to wash her hands. She pulls up her sleeves to expose her elbows. First, she wet her hands and forearms up to and including the elbow. Then she lathers up and rinses, noticing a picture on the wall that is askew. She takes the towel and dries it off, placing the towel back perfectly on the towel ring. She backs out of the bathroom, steps back in, and starts to rewash her hands and forearms, first with the rinse, lather, rinse, and wipe dry.

"Mother, the picture of the sailboat was crooked again. Please watch that when you clean," Stevie returns to the table and sits down, but her shirt is tucked in on one side and not the other. So, she stands up again and adjusts her clothing, then sits.

"Oh, my God, Mom, what's wrapped up on the living room floor?" Stevie asks, aghast.

"I ordered a new rug for the living room floor. It's beautiful. I'll have it out by the time you get home from school," Morgan replies.

"It's country blue," Stevie is horrified. "You know I can't have things that are country blue around me. Make it disappear, please?" Stevie stands still, shaking her hands repeatedly.

"It's beautiful. Maybe take a look at it first?" Mom asks.

"No country blue or Wedgwood blue," Stevie is stunned. "I was adamant about those colors, Mom." Stevie cries while scratching her head.

"I just wanted to liven up the living room with a little blue," Morgan rebuts.

"There are a dozen other acceptable blues: cerulean, primrose, azure, midnight. Why didn't you look for a different shade?"

"Okay, Stevie, we're late now."

"Oh my god, oh my god. I can't go to school now." Stevie stands still, refusing to move.

"Then I have to take Piper. Come on, sweetie. Grab your backpack," Morgan says.

"Mom, you can't leave me home alone with this

Wedgwood rug," Stevie is persistent.

"Well. I'm late. And I don't know what to do?" Mom is searching for an answer.

"I can't go to school late because everything will be ruined. And I can't stay here with that," Stevie points and gags.

"Then come with me. We'll drop Piper off at school; then I'll work to return the rug."

"I'm driving," Stevie says, grabs the keys from the front entry table, and wipes them down with the baby wipes sitting beside them. Before she leaves, she uses the back of her fingers to stroke some feng shui coins on a red string nailed to the door trim eight times. Meanwhile, Morgan and Piper wait for her to finish. Still holding a baby wipe from the front entry, Stevie uses it to clean the SUV door handle before climbing inside.

Once in the SUV, Stevie uses the baby wipes in the console to wipe down the steering wheel. The drive to drop Piper off is uneventful, but Stevie is sure that she ran over someone or something on the return home. She circles the block eight times. On the last turn, a patrol car follows them the rest of the way home. When they exit the SUV, Stevie rushes to enter the house while Morgan stops to talk to the policewoman blocking the driveway with her patrol car.

"I noticed you drove around the block back there a few times. Was there something wrong?" the officer asks.

"No. It's my daughter. She has these quirks when she thinks she runs over something and has to return to check, double-check, and triple-check to see if there is a critter in the road or something."

Morgan is embarrassed and turns to see Stevie repeatedly stepping up and down the stoop, waiting for Morgan to unlock the door. Morgan closes her eyes and sighs.

"Ah, I get it. My nephew has autism spectrum disorder," the policewoman responds. "I'll let you get back to your kid. She looks like she needs you up there."

"Yes, thank you, officer," Morgan replies, walks up the sidewalk, and ascends the stoop steps. "Stevie, you need to stop and talk to police officers to see what they want. Do you hear me? This is important now. Are you listening to me?"

"Yes, about the rug. When will it be gone?" Stevie is curious.

"I'll drag it into the SUV and return it to the store when I go shopping in a little bit. Stop focusing on the rug and get some school work done today."

May 15th, 11:36 am
Basement Bedroom
Dear Journal,

Dad wants me to record my focused intentions so I can learn how to handle them better.

1. The wrong-colored rug in Wedgwood blue made me angry and fearful. What does country blue remind me of? I should know this.

2. Drove over something that skittered off before we returned to remove it from the road, so nobody got hurt. I went around eight times and couldn't find anything. Police followed us home because of it.

3. Didn't talk to the policeman. Apparently, that's a bad thing. I have to learn how to speak to a cop even though I'm in distress with my alignments, aversions, or attention to numbers.

4. Couldn't open the door handle, so I kept counting in multiples of eight until Mom arrived to unlock it. Remember to always have a bag of baby wipes with you for emergencies like this one.

5. Descending the stairs, I found a twisty tie that someone could've tripped over and been hurt. So, I picked it up, then vacuumed, cleaned the vacuum cleaner, and then washed my hands, all of which took two hours.

I'm hungry but don't want to go upstairs until I know Mom has taken care of that rug because it was physically making me sick looking at it. I overheard Mom calling into the attendance line and eavesdropped when the high school receptionist called to verify my illness for today. I have to try and push through times like this morning because people are starting to notice and think that I am eccentric or something. I hear keys and footsteps. Maybe I can go up and get some lunch now.

"Mom," Stevie yells up the stairwell. "Is the rug gone?"

"Yes, Stevie. It's gone," Morgan replies. "I called the school. That wasn't the receptionist who called back this time. It was the school nurse, and she wants me to take you to the doctor and get a referral for a psychiatrist."

"No. I'm not crazy, so I'm not going to do that; you can't make me," Stevie spurts.

"Sweetie, they can make you because you've missed a lot of days this year, unless you want to go to summer school. That might be an option. But the psychotherapy might be helpful," Morgan suggests.

"I won't do either. No. I'm not going to see a shrink, and I'm definitely not going to summer school," Stevie stammers.

"Sweetie, this isn't going to be up to your dad or me. The school can require one or the other of you. If we can't control what they want, I don't know what they'll do. I suppose they could have you hospitalized to have a psychiatrist talk with you. The nurse made this sound very serious. Today crossed some sort of line for them," Morgan elaborates. "I have three days to set up the appointment with our family practice doctor to request the referral. Just be aware of this."

"Daddy can do something," Stevie cries.

"No, he can't. I just want you to be aware that when I tell your dad about this, he's probably going to think that it's a good idea because he's brought it up in the past week."

"No. Mom. No," Stevie bawls uncontrollably. "I'm sorry. I'll try harder. I'll get up earlier, so there's enough time for me to do everything and be on time for school. I promise."

After lunch, Stevie went down to her basement bedroom to power up her laptop to complete some assignments the teachers sent her by email. At which time she noticed an email from one of her best friends.

To: Stevie Mathews
From: Nicolas Montgomery
CC: Isadora Madsen
Subject: Sway, Godsey, and Zwirdle

What happened to you? I'm writing an email because it makes me appear to be working as opposed to goofing off. I'm stuck in Bio with the tawdry triplets. They are nothing short of histrionic as usual. Shawna broke a nail, causing Heidi and Jade to nearly faint. Imagine when we cut up our baby pig for finals?

Stevie takes an open-book Economics test, which is more complex than it sounds, and takes nearly the entire hour. Then it's on to Biology worksheets, English vocabulary self-quiz, and a Spanish grammar packet. Afterward, she returns to her email.

To: Nicolas Montgomery
From: Isadora Madsen
CC: Stevie Mathews
Subject: Re: Sway, Godsey, and Zwirdle

Don't worry. In just three short weeks, we'll be rid of them for the summer. I hate emailing in class. IMO, it'd be so much better, and I could pay so much more attention to what they're saying if they let us text.

Stevie goes into her bathroom to wash her hands and instead gets caught up undressing and checking her body for any sign of lymphoma, melanoma, or other marks.

To: Isadora Madsen
From: Stevie Mathews
CC: Nicolas Montgomery
Subject: summer school vs. shrink

I found out that I either have to attend summer school or get a referral for a shrink because I missed school today.

"Stevie, I'm going to the grocery store. It would help if you came along. Finish your homework when we return," Morgan yells down the stairwell from the kitchen.

"Fine, we need more baby wipes and lint rollers," Stevie says.

"Do you want to drive?" Morgan asks.

"Of course," Stevie responds. "Why wouldn't I want to drive?"

"I just thought maybe this morning with the policewoman may have frightened you," Morgan replies.

"Not at all," Stevie responds while using baby wipes to clean the keys, then her hands. Before she exits the door, she strokes the feng shui coins precisely eight times before rushing out to the car to use the baby wipe to open the handle.

"Pull in this spot. It's closer to the front of the store. Stevie?" Morgan suggests a parking spot, but her daughter goes her own way and parks at the back of the lot, pulling in and backing two and a half times.

Once inside the store, Morgan chooses their vegetables first while Stevie picks out some fruits, one of which is grapes. She puts a grape in her mouth, then asks her mom if she'd like one.

"Stevie, don't do that. Stop eating the grapes. That's stealing," Morgan admonishes while pointing a finger.

Stevie drops the fruit in the cart and stares blankly at her mother.

"Stevie," Morgan is stunned. "You're going to bruise all the fruit. Stop that."

Morgan stares at her daughter, who looks as if she has frozen in place.

Stevie goes from barely breathing to rapid breathing in a matter of seconds. She raises her hands in the air and turns them side to side for everyone to see. Morgan slaps her daughter's hands down, but they pop right up again. They're straight in the air.

"Stevie, what the hell are you doing?" Morgan is curious. She looks around at all the other customers staring at them. "Put your hands down right now. I'm ordering you. What the hell is your problem? You look like you just saw a ghost."

"I don't want anybody to think that I'm stealing," Stevie says.

"Very funny. Stop it," Morgan demands.

"I'm serious, Mom. I don't want them to think that I stole anything. I'll show the cashier under my shirt when we get to the register," Stevie explains. "That way, they can tell for sure that I didn't take anything from them."

"Stevie, I'm sorry for snapping at you back there about the grape. It was one grape. I shouldn't have made a big deal," Morgan explains.

"Stealing is bad, Mom," Stevie agrees. "We need to pay for that grape."

"I will, sweetie. Now, please put down your hands. I think that you're scaring the other customers." Morgan alerts, then adds, "I know for certain that you're scaring me."

"Mom, do I scare you?"

"No, sweetie. That's not what I meant. Let's get the rest of the groceries so we can check out and get the hell out of here," Morgan mumbles the last part so her daughter can't hear.

Once at the register, Stevie takes two quarters out of her pocket and hands them to the cashier. "I ate a grape in the store. I just wanted to make sure that I pay for it."

"That's not necessary," the cashier replies with a smile.

"Please take the damn money," Morgan requests and massages her eyebrows.

"Oh, okay. I'll leave it up here in case somebody else is short of change," the cashier says begrudgingly.

"No, it's payment for the grape I ate. The money belongs in your cash register," Stevie demands. "You need to put it in your change drawer."

"Please, put the coins in your drawer," Morgan says succinctly. "There, you paid for the grapes. Now put your hands down, Stevie."

"I don't want them to think that I stole anything. You can look under my shirt. Go ahead." Stevie tells the clerk.

"No, that's okay," the clerk replies.

"Seriously, I'm fine with it. Mom, it's okay, right?" Stevie asks.

Morgan slaps her daughter's hands from lifting her shirt.

"Ow," Stevie says. "What did you do that for, Mom?"

"Stevie—"

"Oh, no, Mom, we forgot baby wipes and lint rollers. I'll go get them," Stevie says, running through the store with her hands in the air.

When Stevie returns in a rush, the customers behind them are moved over to a new register that has opened, but they're all watching Stevie, whose hands are still upright in the air. She takes out four dimes and two nickels and gives them to the cashier.

"What's this for?" the cashier wonders.

"It's for the grapes," Stevie says matter-of-factly, glaring at the cashier.

"I can't take any more money for the grapes," the clerk says, confused.

"You have to, or I have to do it again," Stevie is adamant.

"She's not kidding," Morgan mumbles, pursing her lips.

"Okay, okay, I'm taking the change and putting it in the drawer," the clerk says, looking afraid.

A manager walks over and asks if there's a problem. Everyone shrugs and shakes their head.

2 Stealing Souls

"Why is Stevie repeating a phone number?" Liam asks Morgan, who is standing at the kitchen island with her hands on her temples.

"Stevie's school wants her to see a psychiatrist or attend summer school."

"What are you going to do?" Liam wonders.

"Me?"

"What are we going to do?" Liam rephrases.

"Obviously, she doesn't want either," Morgan informs.

"Whose phone number is she repeating?"

"Oh, that's just an HVAC business she saw on the side of a truck," Morgan replies.

"So, the school just called you out of the blue, or did something happen at school?"

"She never made it to school because we ran late because she was washing her goddamn hands for so long. Then there was the blue rug."

"Oh, yeah, I wanted to see how that—"

"I returned it to the store today. That was enjoyable since the thing weighed fifty pounds and was bulky and awkward."

"Tell me you're joking," Liam asks. "Why did you cave into her demands?"

"It takes less time and energy than fighting with her," Morgan responds.

"What was wrong with it?" Liam drops his chin to his chest.

"It was country blue," Morgan explains. "I don't know what's wrong with the color. My brother and his wife have the same Wedgwood blue all over their kitchen and dining room hutch."

"We need to stop living like prisoners in this house," Liam begs. "Please tell me that you will stop caving into her whims. Maybe it's best if she sees a shrink."

"Best for who? You?" Morgan blurts while pouring a glass of wine for both of them.

"Best for all of us, especially Piper. I worry that she is processing all Stevie's quirks as normal."

Besides going through three place settings of silverware and two glasses, dinner is uneventful for the majority of them. They do have to watch how excruciatingly slow Stevie is separating her vegetables on the different sides of her plate. Most of the conversation revolves around Piper's class field trip to the science museum.

After dinner, Morgan excuses Stevie to go finish up her homework to avoid another cleaning chemical fiasco. Either that or rogue water spraying off in Stevie's direction. Instead, Stevie chooses to make a list of the license plate numbers that she remembers from the day. After that, she starts a list of places to apply for summer jobs. While doing so, her email pings.

To: Stevie Mathews
From: Nicolas Montgomery
CC: Isadora Madsen
Subject: Where R U?

I'm still trying to reach you by phone, but you haven't texted me all day. What's up?

Stevie goes in to take a shower. The time on the digital clock on the nightstand reads 7:15 pm. The steam from the shower covers the mirror and the barely visible 9:02 pm on the wall clock in the bathroom

To: Nicolas Montgomery
From: Isadora Madsen
CC: Stevie Mathews
Subject: Re: Where R U?

Is this about the shrink? And missing school?
Maybe she got in trouble?

When Stevie returns to her bedroom, she knocks over a pen cup, and one of the pens leaks onto the carpet. She gets hyper and rushes to get a washcloth to clean the ink before it sets in. It's a small spot, but it unnerves her. She scrubs it with bar soap and shampoo. Stevie bawls the whole time and rocks back and forth

To: Isadora Madsen
From: Stevie Mathews
CC: Nicolas Montgomery
Subject: Re: Where R U?

My mom took my phone away today. I won't get it back until after the shrink says it's okay. I kind of put my mom through the wringer today. She doesn't deserve it. Nobody deserves it. I should just kill myself and make it easier for everybody else. Wait. I got to go. Someone is coming down the stairs.

Mom opens up Stevie's bedroom door to find Stevie at the desk, crying.

"Stevie, I'm going to give you an over-the-counter sleep aid," Morgan comforts.

"Just a minute, Mom. Let me put this radon test kit back in its envelope so you can mail it back in the morning," Stevie checks to make certain that it has the correct postage. Then she checks again. And again.

"Why are all of your clothes folded in a pile on a drop cloth on your closet floor?"

"I thought the closet should be color-coordinated," Stevie replies.

"What is with the deck of playing cards standing upright on all the different shelves?"

"It's so I can keep track of when a certain sweater or jeans has been moved," Stevie says.

"To what end, darling?" Morgan asks. "Come and sit here by me." Morgan nearly sits on the bed when Stevie yells.

"No. you need to use the lint roller on your clothes and baby wipes on your hands before you can sit on my bed," Stevie informs.

"Never mind. I'm just worried about you, dear. All these rules must be incredibly consuming of your mind. Maybe on Thursday, when we get in to see our family practice doctor, he'll give an immediate referral to a psychiatrist who can tell us what is happening."

May 15th, 11:36 pm
Basement Bedroom
Dear Journal,

What is happening to me? I'm scared. I'm making all these lists, and it's made me so tired. The image of that car that clipped the curb is imprinted on my mind. I can't stop seeing it and the license plate. So, it must be important in the grand scheme of things.

Mom came down to check on me just now, and I chased her away by requiring her to be clean before she could sit on my bed. Then, when she went to kiss me, I pulled away for fear of germs.

Now I need to examine the best ways to color-coordinate my closet. All by color or pants by color, dresses by color, sweaters by color: as I'm saying it to myself, I think that is the best possible scenario.

Today has been more difficult than other days recently. I've got so much more to do. All the memorizing until I can make lists. I need to go online and use Mom's account to order office supplies.

I need post-it notes in at least eight different colors. Then, I use small tape flags for all the essential notes I need to take from the books I'm reading.

That reminds me. I should check the due dates on that stack of books I checked out from the library the other day

On Thursday, I should get the referral to a shrink who can analyze and diagnose me for the better. For all of us.

The next morning, Stevie wakes an hour early to make certain that she performs all her rituals and is out in the car in time for the drive to school. Izzy waits to greet her. At the door, it's Izzy who opens it and holds it for Stevie. Before they head to homeroom, Izzy uses the bathroom, and Stevie waits for her by the air dryers, but inadvertently gets splashed by an unintentional spray. So Stevie rolls up her sleeves and washes up to and including her elbows.

"Oh, my god, take a bath, why don't you?" Shawna Sway, Stevie's arch-nemesis, recoils.

"Do you have issues? Or what the hell?" Heidi Godsey balks.

"I think you need help," Jade Zwirdle chimes in with her best friends as they laugh at Stevie.

"Go to hell," Izzy snaps upon exiting the bathroom stall.

Just as Stevie is about to move over to under the air dryers, her backpack slides off her shoulder and onto the bathroom floor.

"No," Stevie is distraught, "What do I do with it now?"

"Get the hell out of here. There's nothing to see," Izzy gestures the tawdry trio out the door. "Just wipe it down with some toilet paper, and let's go to homeroom. The bell is about to ring."

"You go ahead. This is going to take a little bit of time," Stevie waves off her best friend.

Izzy waits reluctantly until the bell sounds, then she dashes. Meanwhile, Stevie leaves her backpack where it fell and reaches inside, and takes out cleaning gloves. She enters a stall to get some toilet paper to wet and rinse down the bottom of her backpack, which she then holds up to the air dryer. Keeping the blue gloves on, she leaves the restroom and enters her homeroom class, where students are listening to the day's announcements over the intercom. The entire class stares at Stevie and her gloves as she digs for a baby wipe in her backpack, but she must've left them in the car. So, Stevie goes to the teacher's desk, takes a tissue out of the box, and proceeds to wipe down her desk very carefully before sitting in it.

Garnering the attention of the teacher as well, Stevie notices that he's gesturing for her to talk to him at his desk.

"Hi, there," Stevie says.

"Hello, Stevie," Mr. Gilbert, the homeroom teacher, asks, "Is everything okay?"

"Yes, why?" Stevie is befuddled at the extra attention she gets.

"Stevie, why the gloves?" Mr. Gilbert whispers. "The cleaning staff wipes down every table at night. The desks are clean."

"Is it a problem for me to wipe down the desk?" Stevie is curious.

"Will you be doing that at each one of your classes today?" Mr. Gilbert whispers.

"Yes, can I take some extra tissues? I guess I forgot my baby wipes in the car."

"Stevie, get your backpack and follow me, please," Mr. Gilbert stands up and addresses the class. "Behave for five minutes, and I'll be right back." He gestures to Stevie to exit before him, and she does.

"What's the problem?" Stevie asks once out in the hall.

"Follow me down to the office, please," Mr. Gilbert says.

"What did I do wrong?"

"Nothing, Stevie, just please follow me," he says again.

"Ms. Daniels, can I see you in your office for a second?" Mr. Gilbert asks the school nurse standing behind the receptionist's desk.

"Sure, Mr. Gilbert. Stevie, why are you wearing cleaning gloves?" Ms. Daniels asks, but chooses instead to follow him into her office. "What's happening?"

"She plans on wiping down each desk she sits in throughout the day. The other students are going to eat her alive. Maybe she should see someone before she returns to class. I worry that this is the tip of the iceberg, if you know what I mean?" Mr. Gilbert elaborates.

"I understand completely. Thank you for bringing this to my attention. I'll chat with Stevie now," the nurse says and opens the door for Mr. Gilbert to exit. Stevie enters reluctantly.

"What did I do wrong?" Stevie begins to cry and wipes down the chair before plopping down with a backpack in hand.

"Sweetie, I'm going to call your mother and have her get you in to see your doctor today, okay. I'll be right back." Ms. Daniels leaves for the adjacent office to make the phone call. When she returns, all she has to say is, "Your mother is on her way. You can sit here and wait for her, okay?"

Stevie acknowledges as the bell sounds and students are off to first-hour classes. Stevie sees Izzy peek in the main office's window. They wave to each other.

Once in the SUV, Stevie sits in the driver's seat, embarrassed, "I'm a freak. They don't want me around the other students."

"No, sweetie. This was for your benefit because teenagers can be cruel. With the nurse's referral to our family doctor, we should be able to get in this afternoon. I'll call as soon as we get home, dear," Morgan says.

Two blocks from home, Stevie swerves to miss something in the road and runs over a dog chew toy. She stops, gets out, and looks at it. After she returns to the driver's seat, she gets out again to look at it. She does this a total of eight times while traffic slows in either direction to watch her.

Meanwhile, Mom is on the phone, "Yes, this is Morgan Mathews again. I need to get that appointment pushed up to this afternoon." Morgan peeks out at Stevie and adds, "Actually, anytime today would work. If you've got an immediate appointment, then we'll take it."

"Mom, what are you doing?" Stevie settles in and buckles up.

"The school nurse said that she'd contact you to let you know the importance of this visit. We need to see Dr. Herzing today," Morgan demands. "Thank you. We'll be right there."

Once in the doctor's office waiting room, everyone stares at Stevie cleaning off the chair with the baby wipes she recovered in the car. Then Stevie sits and stands a total of eight times before tapping her fingernails eight times each on the wooden armrest. The receptionist stares while Morgan fills out paperwork for this visit. Once Morgan pays the copay, the nurse takes Stevie back immediately. Morgan joins her.

"They didn't want me out there with the normal people. So they found an empty room for us to wait in," Stevie perceives.

"Whatever the reason, we're here now," Morgan reassures. "Things will be better soon, one way or another."

"Morgan, Stevie? What brings you guys in today?" Dr. Herzing asks upon entering, staring at Stevie.

"Stevie is doing these rituals or actions a certain number of times, a certain way, and she can't stop. Her aversions to smells, cleaning chemicals, even colors are worsening as each hour passes, it seems," Morgan blurts. "Something's wrong. We need help."

"Stevie, how are you doing? You tell me how you're feeling right now,' Dr. Herzing stares straight into her eyes.

"Well, physically, I feel fine," Stevie says.

"No recent head injuries?" Herzing wonders.

"No, but I do have bad headaches," Stevie reveals. "It's just I have to do things a certain number of times, or my family will be killed, or I might kill them accidentally."

"How would you accidentally kill them, Stevie? Tell me," Herzing wonders.

"I don't know. Knives, scissors, or put rat poison in the sugar jar by accident. I don't plan on it."

Herzing notes this in the computer after a back-and-forth glance with Morgan. He shakes his head.

"Who else is going to kill your family?"

"I don't know. Someone will. They'll just die if I don't perform these different actions."

"And can you stop doing these actions so we can see what happens?" Herzing asks.

Stevie starts streaming tears, "I can't stop."

"Okay. Okay. Stevie, are you hearing things that are telling you to do stuff?"

"No."

"Are you seeing things that aren't there?"

"I keep seeing this image in my mind of breaking glass falling down on me, and the shards are pointed and come crashing down. The glass is country blue," Stevie replies.

"And that is bad?" Herzing takes notes on the computer at the desk in the corner.

"I hate country blue. My mom calls it Wedgwood blue."

"Sure, I'm familiar with that color. Why do you think that color bothers you?" Herzing prods.

"I just get nauseated, dizzy, and sweaty. I hate that color."

"Since when?" Herzing delves.

"I don't think that I've ever liked that shade of blue, but I'd say last month, it really started to bother me. Now it's just out of the question. We can't have that color in the house," Stevie explains.

"I had to return a bulky rug because it was that color and waiting to be laid out in our living room," Morgan interjects.

"So you're giving in to Stevie's demands for

order on her terms?" Herzing notes.

"I'm sorry. It just takes less time and energy than arguing with her," Morgan sniffles.

"How is that on your relationship with your husband?"

"Not good. This has been coming on for a year now."

"I'm worried that they'll get a divorce and take my sister away from me," Stevie cries.

"Is that happening?" Herzing asks.

"Oh, god no," Morgan is alarmed.

"I heard you and Dad. You don't want Piper to learn what I'm doing and do it too," Stevie adds. "Dad is angry with you for helping me."

"I'm not helping you, exactly," Morgan defers, "Doctor, what can we do to make this go away?"

"Well, I'll get you in to see a psychiatrist this week, but in the meantime, staying home from school is probably the best thing, but I don't hear intent.

May 16th, 1:24 pm
Basement Bedroom
Dear Journal,

I know that I scared my mom and Dr. Herzing, but it felt good to get it out of my mind. After Dr. Herzing checked me over physically, he had his nurse set up the appointment with the shrink. He told my mom that just like everything else I was doing, thinking, and feeling, the rat poison and sharp objects comment was irrational and should be discounted because everything was based on ritual, accident, and an intense fear of harming. He'll let the shrink diagnose, but it sounds like I have OCD and need medication.

I don't know what's going to happen with the school. Are they going to force me to go to summer school? Will they let me get a doctor's note from this psychiatrist and let me just make up the tests that I'm missing?

My best friends, Nico and Izzy, are looking for summer jobs. I should be out there with them, but I think the plan is to hide me away like dad jokes about a crazy aunt in the attic.

I wonder if that's really where they hid their crazy relatives back then. Are my parents going to be embarrassed about whatever is happening to me? Will they only introduce Piper to their friends?

I'm nervous, and I feel like I need to do something.

"Stevie, are you okay? What's the matter?" Mom asks from where she sits at the desk behind the living room sofa, sketching some designs for the graphic design consulting firm that she telecommutes to and from each day.

"Nothing. I'm just bored. I finished all the homework that the teachers emailed me. The only thing that I'm missing out on are the tests, I guess," Stevie replies. "What are these bags of food still doing unpacked?"

"I'm swamped with work, having missed out on some appointments while we were out," Morgan explains.

"You mean because of me?" Stevie blurts.

"It was important and necessary and had to be done at that moment in time. I'm okay with it. I just didn't get to put the canned and boxed goods in the pantry yet."

"I can do it for you," Stevie offers.

"No, honey, why don't you stay out of the kitchen until dinnertime?" Morgan distracts. "Did you ever finish putting your bedroom closet back together?"

"Mom, I'm not going to poison the sugar jar," Stevie balks.

"No, of course, you're not."

"I mean, we don't even have rat poison, do we?" Stevie says.

Morgan's eyes bulge out, and she combs her fingers through her hair, then pushes her hair behind her ears and walks over to Stevie, who has started emptying out the pantry onto the kitchen counters.

"Look, Mom, it's filthy in here. I'm going to

empty the pantry out, wipe it all down, and put it back together better, in alphabetical order," Stevie says.

"Oh, my god, Stevie. No. Don't do that to yourself. I'll get to cleaning the pantry this weekend, maybe?" Morgan pleads. "Here, let me unload the groceries."

"No, Mom, I already started. I have to finish it my way right now. So please go away," Stevie begs.

It takes about an hour to unload everything stocked in the pantry. Then Stevie uses just a bucket of water with dish soap, the kind they use to clean wildlife after an oil spill, so it's not harmful. She scrubs residue marks and blemishes. Afterward, she takes inventory of what she has to work with and makes a list.

"Should soups go in by brand name, then kind of soup, or just soup?" Stevie thinks aloud. "No soup, brand name, then flavor."

"We're home. I picked Piper up at school. Hon, what's going on in here?" Liam wonders as he and his youngest daughter enter from the garage and mudroom to join Morgan in awe over the mess outside the pantry and covering the counter, island, and table.

"Hi, Dad, I'm reorganizing the pantry for us. It was dusty and dirty, so I'm going through and checking expiration dates and wiping everything down before I put it in alphabetical order," Stevie says, beaming from ear to ear.

"Where are we going to eat dinner?" Piper is curious.

"It's okay, sweetie. Why don't we order pizza tonight?" Mom suggests.

"There's a delivery package at the front door. I'll get it," Liam mumbles, looking back to make sure his eyes aren't failing him. When he returns, he says, "It's to you, hon?" He sets the large box on the only edge of the breakfast table left open.

"I don't think that I ordered anything besides the new living room carpet," Morgan opens the box to find a plethora of post-it notes, tape flags, bookmarks, sheet protectors, sheet tabs, and a few dozen sets of colored pens, pencils, and markers. Index cards in a multitude of colors, along with white-out tape, jumbo paper clips, and some small notepads, fall down to the floor when Morgan shakes the box to see to the bottom.

"I didn't order this," Morgan mumbles and looks at Stevie, "Did you order office supplies?"

"Oh, yes. I needed to organize a few things."

"Stevie, this must've cost a fortune," Liam says.

"Dad, I needed it to stop the bad thoughts," Stevie is about to cry.

"What bad thoughts?" Liam wonders.

"I'll tell you. Why don't we let Stevie work on her task? Piper, why don't you go change and finish any homework you may have?

Morgan takes Liam up to their bedroom, where she relays the entire doctor's visit to her husband. He is alarmed by the rat poison, knives, and scissors comment, but equally shaken that the doctor saw fit to send Stevie home until the psychiatrist appointment.

"He said it's just irrational, random thoughts invading Stevie's mind that make her want to control the situation, so in doing so, she's organizing, straightening, and doing these weird rituals where she taps or strokes coins or keys," Morgan iterates.

Pizza dinner is hypervigilant, considering Stevie has to monitor everyone's food and beverages in the formal dining room off the front entry. At one point, Piper spills her juice, and Stevie nearly has a panic attack.

Three days and two nights go by, with Stevie cleaning and organizing cupboards and closets without much sleep.

When it's time for the psychiatrist's appointment, Liam goes anxiously.

"Hello. I'm Dr. Williams. And you must be Stevie," the psychiatrist greets upon entering. "And Stevie's parents?"

"Yes, sir. Liam and Morgan Mathews. Here for our daughter."

"So, tell me why you're here, Stevie."

"I'm tired from doing things like counting and straightening, but I can't stop because something bad will happen to my family or somebody else if I fail."

"Have you missed school or lost sleep over this?" Dr. Williams wonders.

"Both," Stevie begins crying. "I feel like my body is off physically."

"How do you mean?" the doctor asks.

"My right side feels heavier than my left, both in the legs and in the arms. I feel off. Everything around me feels chaotic. I have to focus on things, or bad images flash across my mind. Terrible things like my family getting killed."

"Do you want to kill your family?"

"No."

"Do you want to harm yourself?"

"No."

"What changes have you as parents seen in your daughter, and when did this start?" Dr. Williams addresses Liam and Morgan.

"About a year ago, I noticed more attention to detail, but it came and went. Then she went through a feng shui phase where she hung these lucky coins on a red string atop the trim on our front door. That was about six months ago. Then, early last month, she began stroking the coins with the back of her fingers a few times. Suddenly it turned to eight times with that, and then other things. Always eight. A few weeks ago, she started making lists of random phone numbers and license plates of vehicles. Then she'd repeat odd words or phrases. Now she's doing these rituals with a deck of playing cards in the closets she organizes."

"Mr. Mathews?"

Liam starts crying. He looks everywhere in the room, but the tears stream down his face. "I'm scared for my daughter, both of them. I watch Stevie struggle with symmetry, alignment, and ritual, and I worry that our younger daughter will get it, too."

"Are you scared of your daughter?" Dr. Williams asks.

Liam bawls into his hands. "Something took our little girl from us. It just ripped her from our grasp and left this shell. If it's that difficult for me to watch, then it must be terrifying for Stevie to go through. I love my daughter and want her back."

3 Sidewalk Love Letters

"If my own dad is scared of me, how do other people feel. Like at the grocery store and at school, when they run into someone like me?"

"You can only do the best you can, Stevie," Dr. Williams says. "And we're going to do our best to make it, so you don't have to do these compulsions or have these obsessions, or at least lessen the extent so you can live a more normal life."

"Great, how do I do that?"

"Well, it is a combination of medicine specifically for people with obsessive-compulsive disorder and psychotherapy that includes a type of cognitive-behavioral therapy known as exposure response prevention."

"And that helps people like me?"

"We've had very pleasing results," Dr. Williams adds. "The only obstacle is time. It can take weeks for the medicine to work, and that's if we have the correct one at the optimal dosage. Different medicines work differently on different people. Plus, psychotherapy takes a great deal of time in appointments. Initially, I think we want to start you out three times a week. Then, after a few weeks, when the medicine kicks in, go down to two appointments a week, then lower it accordingly. I realize that may not be what you want to hear, but I want to be honest with you, all of you."

"So, do we start today?" Morgan inquires.

"Based on the notes I received from your clinic, the packet you filled out online, and my own observations, I think that we can and should get you in tomorrow. It's already late in the day for today.

Plus, psychologists or therapists like to read a little background data before they jump in with a new client. So we'll get this logged, and I think Shelby will be a perfect match for you."

"She's the psychologist?" Liam asks.

"I believe Shelby is a Licensed Marriage and Family Counselor with somewhere near twenty years of experience, many of them with the younger population and a great deal of them with Obsessive-Compulsive Disorder. In fact, she runs our group counseling on Thursday nights." Dr. Williams elaborates.

"Am I going to group counseling tonight?"

"No. Shelby will need to spend some time with you before you're ready for group work," Dr. Williams responds.

"Today, I'll be putting you on two medications: one for OCD and the other for anxiety, which both your family practice doctor and I think is necessary initially. One acts rather quickly, and the other takes a few weeks to show results. Then a few weeks from now, we'll meet back here and discuss any progress or unlikely side effects," the doctor surmises.

"So, is she supposed to go back to school tomorrow?" Morgan wonders.

"Actually, one more day off to see the effects of the first medicine's immediate results, which will also give you a chance to get in to see Shelby during office hours that she has available on short notice." Dr. Williams replies.

After leaving the counseling center, they stop by the drugstore drive-thru to pick up the prescriptions emailed over by the psychiatrist. Morgan hands Stevie the prescribed amount to take, then they make their way through the remaining fifteen minutes through heavy traffic. By the time they enter the garage, Morgan looks at Stevie, who is nearly asleep in the back seat of the SUV.

"Oh, my god, Liam," Morgan alerts. "The pills have knocked her out. Do you think he prescribed the correct amount? Or maybe the pharmacy made a mistake and gave her someone else's prescription?"

"We'll verify the bottle information on the handouts they gave us at the clinic. I think the nurse said there's somewhere we can go online to check to make certain that the correct medication is dispensed. I'm pretty certain they know what they're doing, Morgan."

Stevie is still mildly cognizant of what's being said about her. "I can hear you guys. I'm right here."

"Good, then you think you can still walk inside, or do you need me to carry you?" Dad asks.

"I'm good. I think," Stevie replies. Her eyes droop, and a little drool drips.

"Wait for me, Stevie. I want to help hold you up when you get out. Let me come around."

Dad rushes to get Stevie, who exits the SUV and leans forward into it for support. Mom gets the doors, and Dad guides Stevie down to her basement bedroom and sets her down gently on her bed while Mom pulls off her shoes and covers her up with a throw from the armchair near the window.

Dad excuses himself upstairs to his laptop on the kitchen counter, where he starts researching what type of pills they prescribed his daughter. Meanwhile, Morgan continues to check on Stevie's breathing to make sure they didn't give their child a catastrophic dose.

"It lists drowsiness as a side effect, Morgan. Plus dizziness, sweating, and upset stomach. So don't be too surprised if she doesn't feel like eating tonight, honey." Liam warns, then adds, "Are you getting Piper from school, or am I?

"Would you get her? I'm apprehensive about Stevie and want to keep checking on her."

When Liam returns with Piper, she takes a snack up to her bedroom to do her homework, and Liam gets back to his research.

"I think they hit the nail on the head with this diagnosis, honey. It really sounds like what Stevie has been going through. I feel like a jerk for joking about this disorder when it is so painful for so many people. Coworkers are always like, 'You are so OCD,' when someone is overly organized, but it could be that they have a milder form of what Stevie has. Like I said, I feel like a jerk knowing this is now happening to our daughter," Liam says.

"Well, I always knew about OCD's obsessive organizing and rigidity with certain things, but this seemed like a whole other category. Stevie has been in physical discomfort due to this," Morgan replies.

"All or nothing thinking, catastrophizing, selective attention, magical or superstitious thinking with thought-action or thought-event fusion is what it lists. This is what Stevie has, definitely. Now we just need to follow through on the psychiatrist's suggestions. Are you going to be able to take off work to take Stevie in tomorrow morning?" Liam asks.

"As long as you can take Piper to school, this should work out for us tomorrow at least. It might get trickier with the number of appointments she'll have initially." Morgan replies, then adds. "Did you get the impression that the doctor made it sound like Stevie was a top-tier case?"

"Yeah, I did," Liam responds. "But I think we may have found the right doctor off the bat. At least, I hope so."

Morgan continues her checks on Stevie every half hour through the night. Stevie is knocked out. Every so often, she readjusts her head, but she doesn't even change positions in bed. She's lying exactly as she was placed earlier. Morgan takes a wet wipe, washes away some sweat from her daughter's forehead, and pulls back the blanket.

"Mom, I'm thirsty," Stevie says around 6:45 am the following day.

"It's a clean glass, darling," Morgan promises.

"Did I have dinner last night?" Stevie is curious about the chain of events.

"No," Morgan says. "You were pretty much out for the count within fifteen minutes of me giving you the prescription, sweetie."

"I think the pills are maybe wearing off because I'm getting thoughts again. How long until my next dose, Mom?"

"Well, we have an appointment with the therapist first thing today. I don't want you to sleep through that, so I don't want to give you the medication until you meet with her," Mom says.

"Okay. But I'm hungry. Can I eat?"

"Certainly," Mom responds and takes her daughter up to make her breakfast. Dad and Piper join in after a short while. Then Stevie returns to her bedroom to shower and dress for the appointment.

"I think positive results are happening from one or both of the medications. Stevie's anxiety isn't as high as it was. And she didn't do the morning rituals prior to eating," Morgan says.

"Yeah, I noticed that, but didn't want to bring it up. Can we really be this fortunate to have found a cure?"

"I think they said that it's never cured, but with the ongoing focus on medication and behavior management, we might have our wish for the worst to be over," Morgan is giddy.

Dad and Piper take off for work and school while Mom waits for Stevie to reappear from the basement. Unfortunately, Stevie is doing the rituals again and, without fail, strokes the feng shui coins on the front door eight times before they leave.

"Can I drive, Mom?" Stevie asks.

"You're still under the influence of the medication. So, I'm going to say no this time, darling," Morgan denies Stevie.

"Mom, I think you ran over a squirrel or something," Stevie alerts. She makes Mom drive around eight times to verify that it was only a tiny pothole and not a critter or worse.

When they get to the counseling clinic, Stevie takes out her baby wipes to clean all the door handles, elevator buttons, clipboard, and pen used to fill out the daily inventory of emotions. When Stevie takes a seat both in the waiting room and in the therapist's office, she makes her usual stand and sit eight times compulsively. As they wait for the therapist to take some notes on the emotional inventory, Stevie has to tap her nails on the chair's wooden arms, rub her pant legs, and touch the keys she has taken and wiped with a wet wipe from Mom.

"Are you nervous to see me, Stevie?" Shelby asks.

"Yes, I don't know what to expect," Stevie responds.

"We pretty much do what you want in this room," Shelby says. "I don't think I surprise people that often. I do offer suggestions and my plan, of course, but that's to be expected.'

"Okay," Stevie stops the rubbing and tapping as she takes an opportunity to look around the room at the ambient lighting, personal photos, knick-knacks, and artwork.

"When we get more into cognitive behavioral therapy, I'll give more direction, but for right now, I want to get to know you, Stevie."

"Didn't they send the information about me? The psychiatrist said that he'd give you my information." Stevie is worried.

"Sure, I got the introductory information, but I'd like to just talk with you. So, are you happy with school?"

"Nobody is happy going to school," Stevie says and inadvertently snorts.

"That's probably true."

"How has your illness affected your schooling besides attendance?"

"It's made me the subject of laughter, especially among people who never liked me."

"We all have people that we don't get along with, and you know what: some people we'll never be able to make happy, so maybe we should stop trying and think about the ones that do stand by us despite our problems," Shelby says.

"I think my homeroom teacher is scared of me, just like my dad," Stevie says.

"Your dad told you that he's scared of you?" Shelby asks.

"Yes," Stevie begins crying.

"How did that make you feel?" Shelby notes while watching Stevie.

"It made me feel like a miserable person to make their own parent afraid. I love my dad. I wish that he loved me as much as he loves my sister, Piper, who isn't mentally ill," Stevie says as she starts blinking repeatedly.

"Do you remember the absolute first thing that you obsessed over? When was that? Tell me about the situation," Shelby asks.

"We took a road trip to see my grandma for Thanksgiving last year, and I was in the car, in the backseat with my sister, Piper. She talked to me about something, and I could only pay attention to how many cemeteries we passed. I'd count them and recall one thing that stood out about each cemetery."

"How many cemeteries did you count?" Shelby wonders.

"Sixteen."

"And when was the first time you were concerned about alignment, symmetry, or things being perfect?"

"I got the flu between Thanksgiving and Christmas last year, and I was sick at home, but my friends came by and wrote, 'I Love You' in sidewalk chalk on the walkway in front of our house. It was crooked and country blue."

"Yes, tell me about the country blue. Tell me about what that means to you."

"It made me vomit all day that day, remembering the words on the sidewalk. When I closed my eyes, I still saw it. And when it rains, it mixes with standing snow all over the sidewalk, it makes the chalk letters all jagged and spiky like knives."

"About the knives and scissors that you told the doctor about in reference to hurting your family, tell me about that, please?"

"I see these images in my mind, with my eyes open and closed, and they don't go away. I sit on my hands, so nothing bad happens."

"How often does that happen? How often do these images take over?" Shelby asks.

"Throughout the day, fourteen times yesterday. That was the most so far."

"And do you want to hurt your family?" Shelby asks.

"No. That's why I sit on my hands."

"Okay," Shelby pauses. "At the times you see these images, is your family doing something that makes you angry?"

"Sometimes."

This garners a look between the therapist and Morgan, who's been sitting silently, crying occasionally.

"Give me a specific time. Tell me about it from beginning to end."

"My sister, Piper, was playing with this deck of cards. And she was doing it all wrong. Everything was in disarray or uneven. I kept telling her to fix it, but she wouldn't. So I sat on the sofa and watched her. These images of her being stabbed came into my mind, and they wouldn't go away. So, I had to sit on my hands so nothing bad happened to Piper. I didn't want to lose my sister. So, I went down to my bedroom and started tapping my fingers eight times, then I'd start over again."

"Tell me about another time, Stevie."

"When I go to bed, I do things in a certain order to make sure nothing evil happens to anybody I love. So, one time last week, I was getting ready for bed when Piper came in, and she lay on my bed. It was fixed perfectly for me. It was meant for me. There wasn't a wrinkle on it. Then Piper plopped on the bed and giggled like it was funny. I couldn't stop shaking, and I started pulling the hair from my head. I screamed, but nobody came. Then Piper said something and left. I couldn't hear what she was saying because I was screaming until she got up off my bed."

"Where were your parents?"

"My dad had gone to the store to get mulch and soil for my mom. She was upstairs washing clothes and had her earbuds in. Piper was okay, though. I wouldn't do anything to hurt her. That's why I sit on my hands."

"What happens if you don't sit on your hands?"

Stevie pauses. Tears stream down her cheeks. Morgan starts to cry as well. Shelby excuses herself for one moment and leaves the mother and daughter alone. It's about fifteen minutes before Shelby returns. Stevie and Morgan can hear her whispering in the hallway outside the office door. When she does enter, they see a man in a suit standing outside the door across the hall.

"Our time is going to be up soon. Stevie, if I

could get just one more time, you had these images of your family being hurt," Shelby asks while taking notes on her computer.

"The other day, my mom bought a rug, and it was country blue. I couldn't believe that she'd do that to me. I was so nauseous and dizzy. I just felt like I was standing on the roof and about to fall off. I closed my eyes, and I saw images of my mom being stabbed, then my sister, who was sitting at the table."

"Now, Stevie, remember back to that moment. Do you know if there were any sharp objects around you?"

"Yes, the knife block in the kitchen, and my mom had a red pair of scissors out on the kitchen countertop. She was cutting a recipe out of a magazine before we came into the room for breakfast."

"Did you want to hurt your mother or sister?" Shelby asks.

"No. Definitely not," Stevie swears.

"Did you sit on your hands?" Shelby asks while continuously typing up notes.

"No."

"Did that make it feel like you could hurt your mom?"

"Yes."

"How did the images stop that day?" Shelby pauses to stare at Stevie.

"My mom promised to do what I wanted and return the rug."

"What if she didn't promise to return the rug that day?"

"I don't know. She did."

"But what if she had said no to you? What would you have done?

"I don't know. Cut the rug up. Stab at it as it stood against the wall, all rolled up."

"What else would you stab at?" Shelby doesn't take her eyes off Stevie.

"Nobody. I don't think," Stevie cries uncontrollably.

"Okay, guys, our time is up, but I need to tell you that Dr. Williams has sent an order over to the hospital for you to stay there for three days just so they can watch you."

"No. I can't go to the hospital. I'm scared of hospitals.

"This will be good for you, Stevie. They will monitor you getting started on your medication, and the psychiatrist there will talk with you and relay your status to Dr. Williams, and they'll decide on what's best for you while you get adjusted to your medicine."

"I won't go," Stevie swears. "You can't make me."

"Yes, we can. Dr. Williams has already sent the paperwork over to the hospital. There is going to be an ambulance outside this clinic in the back that will take you over to the hospital," Shelby says.

"Will she be in a special children's unit?" Morgan asks.

"This is just the local hospital. The children's hospital downtown didn't have any open beds. At this local hospital, there is only a psychiatric ward, but all the patients are closely monitored. There are teen group therapy sessions with people the same age. This is just so you start the medication and get leveled off."

"Mom, I took medicine like I was supposed to," Stevie bawls.

"I know, sweetie. But maybe this will be best for a few days. Your dad and I don't know how best to give you the medication, so it doesn't knock you out, yet so that it helps you," Morgan cries. "Please do this for me, sweetie. Your dad and I will be up to see you each day. That is okay, right?" Morgan asks Shelby.

"They have rules that you have to earn visiting privileges. But they do have visiting hours each day for parents."

"Who is that man standing outside your office door?" Stevie asks.

"He's an associate of mine. A fellow therapist who is in between patients can help you get to the ambulance."

"Mom," Stevie stands up and hugs Morgan, then collapses to the floor in uncontrollable tears.

Shelby opens the door, and the other therapist enters. He tries to take Shelby's hand, but she refuses. She lies on the floor crying. Morgan tries to get her to comply, but Stevie doesn't. The therapist lifts Stevie up into his arms and carries her out the door. Shelby follows them down to the back entrance of the building and out into the ambulance. Once in the ambulance, Stevie begins kicking and screaming for her mom and dad. They give her a sedative shot, and in quick order, she calms and closes her eyes.

4 To Chase an Echo

The time on the wall clock in the emergency room lobby reads: 10:21 am.

I'm awake and groggy as hell, being pushed through the hospital corridors by two tall and bigger-than-average male nurses. Oh, great, the ward is locked. Unfortunately, they have badges to gain entry. Now that we are in the locked ward, I see a couple of elderly people separate but pacing the same route up and down the hallways. Most patients are in glass-encased meeting rooms on either side of the main entrance hallway and watch me being wheeled in, strapped to the chair. First up, an exam room adjacent to the nurses' station where I'm to undress, and they inspect me for pills. Nothing. I get hospital pajamas and a robe, and the female nurse doing the examination walks me down to a room, a double. The other patient is gone.

"I'm Rebecca. I'll be your main nurse. I work most days, but I do have an occasional night off. When I'm not here, any one of the other nurses can assist you," she says. "Initially, you'll have to wear hospital pajamas and a robe until you gain privileges on the ward. How do you feel?"

"I'm a little bit out of it, yet. How long am I here for?"

"You are on a three-day hold," nurse Rebecca replies.

"So, I can go home on Monday. Because I have school."

"What medicines have you taken today?"

Rebecca notes.

"Nothing. I don't think. My mom didn't give me the one that makes me sleepy because I had a therapy appointment. I don't know what the ambulance staff gave me."

"Well, I'm going to go and get your medicine. A lab tech might be up to draw your blood while I'm at my desk," Rebecca says.

"What are you doing lab tests to find out?" Stevie asks.

"To determine what's in your system," the nurse responds.

"I'm hungry," Stevie says.

"Lunch is at 11:30 am up here, so pretty soon," Rebecca informs. "I'll be right back."

"Hello, blood draw for the lab," a person in scrubs and a white lab coat says.

After the lab tech leaves, Rebecca returns with the meds and some paperwork. It's all history for things like drug and alcohol use, sexual and physical abuse, and family dynamics, all of which make Stevie uncomfortable, but she answers nonetheless to get some food and street clothing privileges on the ward.

The medication that Rebecca gave her is the same one that she had the previous evening that knocked her out. Now it is making her so sleepy, Stevie can barely walk, but she has to try it regardless to get food. Stevie's got the munchies, so she'd eat about anything at this time. Plus, she's unaware of anybody else in the ward, at her table in the dining room, or even who her roommate is when she returns to her room.

Stevie isn't required to attend the afternoon

group therapies because of sleepiness, but does meet with the hospital psychiatrist for a brief twenty minutes.

"Do you know why you are here?" the psychiatrist asks.

"Because I told the truth and got in trouble for it," Stevie responds.

"We're here to help you," he says.

"I'm afraid to talk," Stevie admits. "You might want to keep me here longer.

"We need you to tell us the truth. We'll monitor you on the meds. And if all is well, you can leave on Monday morning."

"Okay."

"This is best for you and your family. Do you understand?"

"I understand that they're afraid of me now," Stevie says, grabbing a tissue.

"We need to do what we do to protect everybody involved. I understand that you have a younger sister."

"Yes, Piper," Stevie replies with a smile.

"In my experience, most families are resilient and bounce back after the initial diagnosis and first hospital stay," the shrink says.

"Well, I hope they forgive me," Stevie says before she's dismissed for roaming the ward's common areas until dinnertime.

When the bank of landline phones opens up at 4:00 pm, Stevie is one of the first in line to get to use the four wall phones.

"Mom, are you coming to see me tonight?" Stevie asks.

"How are you, sweetie?" Mom says.

"I'm okay."

"I'm sorry that I couldn't do anything to prevent you from being taken there, but it was out of my control," Mom explains.

"It's okay. I'll just try and make it through it," Stevie responds.

"They said that I should bring up some clean clothes for three days."

"Can you also bring my journal and a pen?" Stevie requests.

"I was just told that the psychiatric staff would be providing writing implements, so I'm not to bring a pen or pencil of any sort. And you can only have journals which aren't wire-bound."

"I have a bunch of blank journals on my bookcase."

"Do Dad and Piper know that I'm here?" Stevie is curious.

"Yes, I called your dad after the ambulance took you away."

"And Piper?"

"I told her a short bit ago when I picked her up from school."

"And what do they think?"

"Piper doesn't know any better. So she just thinks you're having a sleepover at a hospital because your mind is overtired and needs to calm down and get used to some medicine."

"And Dad?"

"Your dad is stunned. He just went silent when I told him that they took you away from me," Mom explains.

"Is he even more afraid of me now?"

"Stevie, your dad loves you."

"That means, yes."

"I want you to know how much we both love you and want you well for your sake, sweetie."

"I have to go now. We only get to make short phone calls. And there's a line. Please don't forget about me," Stevie pleads with a tear streaming down her face.

"Sweetie—"

Stevie hangs up the phone and returns to her room for a nap until dinnertime at 5:30 pm. After the commons area, such as the TV room and dining area, is tidied up by the patients, visiting hours begin.

"Stevie," Dad reaches out to hug her, but Stevie is indifferent.

The same goes for Mom.

"Where's Piper?"

"She has a sleepover tonight," Mom replies.

"So you didn't want her to see the crazies like her sister?"

"You're not crazy. This is all part of a disorder that you have. A disorder that is treatable with medication and therapy," Dad says while reaching out for Stevie's hand. She refuses.

"Where are my clothes?"

"They have to go through an inspection process before you get them."

Stevie yawns. "They gave me medication that's wearing off, I think. So I want to go back to my bedroom, so I don't do anything peculiar and get watched any more than I already am." Stevie turns to walk away.

But Dad grabs her and hugs her. She pulls back, "You don't have to be afraid of me anymore. I won't hurt you guys or your daughter."

"Stevie, come back here. I want—"

After all the visitors left, there's a brief snack time, movie time, then vitals and meds are given out, then retreating to the bedrooms, and finally lights out. Stevie's obsessions and compulsions return, and the roommate notices the rituals and the night nurse makes a note of them. The sedating effect of the pills wears off quicker each time. She is just always a little tired and has a dry mouth.

In the morning, after dressing in her own clothes and breakfast, there is a touch base group and then optional weekend therapy groups that are highly encouraged, like separate disorder groups, grief and loss group, AA and NA group, symptom management, yoga, board games, or outside walks around campus for those who have earned the privilege. The phone bank is also open for a couple of hours each morning, afternoon, and evening, with only a ten-minute limit.

"Hey, I'm Molly."

"I'm Stevie."

"You're going to want to attend groups to earn points with the nurses, or they'll never release you," Molly, Stevie's roommate, suggests as they sit across the room from each other. "There's an OCD group for you."

"What makes you think that I need an OCD group?"

"You're sitting down and standing up, tapping your fingers, and rubbing your pant legs repeatedly. The last person in that bed had OCD, too. She went to groups and interacted, and they released her," Molly informs.

"So, what's your story?" Stevie inquires.

"I cut myself because they say I don't know how to deal with emotional pain, frustration, and just overall being pissed off and angry as hell. They brought me in here on suicide watch when I accidentally cut into my wrists too deeply," Molly explains.

"What groups do you attend?"

"The yoga one is good; that's twice each day, once in the morning and another one in the afternoon by a different instructor. Everyone is quiet and keeps to themselves. I attend the self-harm group, the bipolar group, the sexual abuse group, the medication management group, like side effects, group walks, the teen group, and horticulture therapy. We take care of the plants down in the greenhouse in the courtyard. On weekends, they have an animal therapy group where therapy dogs are brought into the gymnasium, and we can play with them for an hour."

"Has your family been up to see you?" Stevie asks.

"I don't have a good relationship with my family like you do," Molly says.

"How do you know that I've got a good relationship?"

"I saw your parents try to hug you when you walked away from them last night. I'm sorry. Everything is out in the open, and we all know each other's business in here for the most part," Molly elaborates.

"My parents let them put me in here. They didn't do anything about it," Stevie fumes.

"Sometimes they can't control the situation,"

Molly says.

"My dad said that he's afraid of me: his own daughter," Stevie wipes a tear from her eyes. "The therapist they took me to got me to say that I've got these persistent images about harming my family. I didn't say that I'd act on them. She tricked me with words. My mother didn't even step in to help. It pissed me off. Now, I'm in here. I'm missing school for all these appointments I have to make to talk to a therapist who has it out for me."

"I think the teen group will be good for you. There are a lot of other angry people in there, too."

"Aren't you angry?"

"Yes, but I take it out on myself. I'm not as mad at the world. I know they want me to be more in touch with the anger and to let it out in the group, but I don't think I'm wired that way," Molly says. "I think I'm in your touch base group with the other teens. Shall we go?"

"Sure, why not?" Stevie is falling into line. "If I have to play along to move on."

"Okay, I guess I'll lead off even though only one person doesn't know me. My name is Jace, and I'm seventeen and in here because I had a depressive episode with my bipolar disorder. I hope to get out sometime this week," Jace, a slim and awkward teen, says.

"I'm Cooper, and I'm in here for a substance abuse problem. Oh, I'm seventeen, too."

"Hi, everyone, I'm Gage. I'm the new girl; I'm sixteen and just lost my dad to a heart attack. So I'm trying to learn how to deal with grief the correct way and not act out."

"I'm Rhiannon, and I'm in here for an eating

disorder, specifically bulimia, and I'm sixteen."

"My name is Bailey, " I said to the new girl. I'm in here for cutting and acute depression. I'm seventeen."

"My name is Molly. And I'm roommates with Stevie here, so she knows about my cutting. I'm seventeen, and I've been in here the longest out of everyone in this room."

"I'm Stevie. I'll be sixteen in a month and a half. I have obsessive-compulsive disorder. I just found out this week. My therapist had me brought here because I'm having images and have to perform rituals."

"Okay, that was good, guys. Now, what's the plan for the day? Everybody in the teen group? Okay. Stevie?" the facilitating nurse, Jackie, asks.

"Yes."

'Great. I'll be overseeing that group as well. So what else is everyone going to do today?"

Cooper says, "I have an AA meeting this morning and this evening."

Rhiannon points to Bailey and says, "We're going to the self-harm group, board games, and movie night."

Gage nods, "I'm in on the board games and movie night, plus I've got grief and loss support group twice today. There's nobody my age in there, but the group is pretty cool."

"I'm up for board games and movie night too, but I want to get some sketching done, and my parents plan to visit, too," Cooper says.

Molly says, "I'm thinking about the medication management group as well as yoga, and of course, the self-harm group."

"I understand there's an OCD group. Plus, if I could join you to the medication management group and yoga, I'd like to," Stevie asks Molly.

Rhiannon asks, "Do you self-harm? You're welcome to come with us, too?"

"I pull my hair out," Stevie asks. "Does that count?"

"Why yes, it does," nurse Jackie says. "Good for everyone here. I'm glad that all of you are making an effort. It's almost time for 9:00 am groups, so we'll get in touch again tomorrow. And good job, guys, all of you."

"Stevie, the self-harm group is down the hall," Rhiannon says, and all the girls leave in that direction.

A handful of adult women join the self-harm group, where the teens enter first and sit next to each other. After brief introductions, they start by talking about cutting, which most of the group does, then eating disorders that four of the group have. Two people put a cigarette out on their skin or use curling irons to burn themselves. Then there are two others besides Stevie that pull their hair out.

"I don't even realize that I'm doing it until I'm finished, and my scalp hurts, and I have a bunch of strands in my hand," Stevie inputs. "And can I ask why there are only females in this group? Is this just a female thing?"

"No, but I don't know if I should speak for the group or other members, but it's common for self-injury patients to attend the sexual abuse group as well. And there aren't many guys in there either, if that tells you anything," a thirty-something patient named Melody says.

After the self-harm group is over, Molly and Stevie return to their bedroom for Stevie to change into yoga pants and a tee. Molly is already dressed in that fashion. They go to the meditation studio where a group was just let out and wait for the yoga instructor and the other attendees. Stevie has to stand and sit eight times and repeatedly does her tapping and rubbing. When Melody from the self-harm class joins them, she uses some hand sanitizer, then takes Stevie's hands in hers and squeezes.

About a half dozen other women from all age ranges join in on the yoga group just before the instructor arrives late, making a couple of people angry. The instructor is profuse about her apology, and things are then okay. The session is seamless. She asks the group how it went.

"It was moderately intense, but I think that's good for the self-harm tendencies. It takes our minds off the compulsion," Melody says.

"It focused my mind on something other than the tapping and rubbing, which is good," Stevie is surprised she responds. "I can't believe I just said that."

"Why?" Melody wonders.

"It's so personal. And I'm typically quiet and pretty shy."

"Being in here is liberating. You just feel free to speak your mind without people judging you," Melody replies. "Where are you guys off to next?"

"Lunch, then the medication management group, and you?" Stevie responds.

"The women's AA group after lunch," Melody leaves but, looking back, waves and says, "Bye."

"I think people find you easy to talk to," Molly

tells Stevie. "Melody has never spoken to me."

"Really," Stevie is surprised.

At lunch, one of the other patients is angry about getting applesauce instead of pudding and making a scene with everyone focusing on most people taking sides as to whether they'd be outraged if they didn't get their pudding. The nurses try to change the subject, but it lingers on for half an hour.

"Are there a lot of incidents like that in here?" Stevie whispers.

"Not many, but some. I think people on the outside think that this place must be violent or something, but I've only seen a few times when nurses had to intervene about someone's anger or frustration," Molly says.

"Really?" Stevie asks.

"I think people come in here to calm down and leave all that mental chaos on the outside," Molly adds.

The medication management group is held in a conference room-type setting with an office table, chairs, and a whiteboard that the nurse facilitates the group to stand at to welcome everybody. She starts by asking if anybody wants to do introductions for the new people in the group, or shall we just move on to the drugs?

"We can introduce ourselves as we ask our questions," an older man says.

"How about that, everyone?" the nurse asks, and everyone nods in reply. "Okay, who wants to start us off?"

"Seroquel kicks my butt," the older man says. "I'm Harvey, and I have paranoid schizophrenia."

"It does that to everybody," an older woman

responds, "My name is Sylvia. Plus, it gives you the munchies. Oh, I have bipolar disorder."

"It pisses me off, too. I really get frustrated about crap. I'm sorry to everyone for the outburst at lunch. But who wants applesauce when you order pudding?" Harvey replies.

"I think the majority was on your side. If you don't feel like applesauce, you don't feel like applesauce. They screwed up." Another older man adds. "I'm Dennis, and I just lost my wife, and my family put me in here because they're worried I'm suicidal. I'm not."

The following three meds up for discussion are of interest to Stevie: clomipramine, fluoxetine, and sertraline. Three different people bring up those medications and discuss the cost, effectiveness, and side effects.

"Clomipramine was prescribed to me as a teenager and worked okay, but fluoxetine really made a difference for my OCD until earlier this year," a young twenty-something says, "Oh, I'm Lucy."

"Citalopram and venlafaxine are two that worked well for my OCD. My problem was combining them with alcohol to get rid of the increased anxiety, shakiness, and terrible insomnia. I'm in here for alcohol addiction, too. And I'm Marvin."

"Hello. I'm Stevie, and I'm also in here for OCD. The two that they have me on, which you already spoke of, don't seem to be working. I mean, they knock me out, but even that seems to be wearing off."

"Your doctor will be switching them up over

and over again until you guys find the right one," Lucy says.

"Yeah, I tried four before finding my workhorses," Marvin adds.

"You should join us in the OCD group. I've found it to have a lot of useful information in it," Lucy welcomes Stevie.

"Yes, I'll do that. Thank you," Stevie replies.

The remainder of the meeting focused on anti-anxiety and anti-depressant medications, which were very interesting as well. Molly spoke up a few times, along with a couple of others in the group, about the depression meds and their side effects. The more boisterous discussion was about anti-anxiety drugs, which are highly addictive and sought out by many but guarded by pharmacists under lock and key. That was the only discussion in the fifty-minute session, which produced tears in a few patients.

After a brief restroom break and grape juice in the dining room with Molly, they part ways, and Stevie returns to the same conference room for the OCD support group and Lucy, Marvin, Alice, Elias, and Henry.

"Shall I start?" Marvin asks the nurse sitting at the head of the table, just listening in and there to answer questions and make sure the group stays on topic, and that everyone gets a turn. She nods her head.

"I'm Marvin, and I have OCD. Obviously, that's why I'm in this group. While my medication works well for my OCD, I have side effects. Anxiety is a bitch. Plus, shakiness and wicked insomnia affect me as well. So I drink to take the edge off, and I guess I get to drinking a little too much, and I'm a depressing drunk that worries my family. They thought it best that I come in for detox and get on the straight and narrow again." Marvin says, then nudges the young guy next to him with his shoulder.

"Hi, I'm Elias, and I just turned seventeen. I was brought in overnight for my OCD and lack of sleep. They gave me a sedative, and I just woke up after lunch was over. I met Marvin here, and he got them to send up a late lunch for me because I was starving. I don't know anything about which meds I'm taking, but I don't think they work since I've been up cleaning and organizing for three nights. I guess I can't think of any more to say," Elias shrugs.

"Alice, here, I just turned thirty. Six months ago, I lost my job to downsizing, and therefore, I lost my health insurance. So, I was off my meds for a few months. So when I got a new job, and the benefits kicked in, I went back to my old doctor, and she prescribed me what I was taking before, but this time around, it didn't work, and these violent and horrific images have plagued me, and I'm on edge because I fear that I'll blurt something out, like swear at people on the train."

"Henry here, I'm twenty-six, and I've got OCD. My doctor says that I've got severe functional impairment, and I need to get on the right track to return to work. My medications used to handle my symptoms, but then I stopped going to therapy, and things just sort of blew up when my girlfriend broke up with me, and I'm in here trying to get stabilized so I can return to my apartment instead of with my parents."

"Hey, all of you. My name is Lucy. I've had

OCD since I was sixteen. I'm twenty-two now. I've started having these horrific images, too, and I'm scared that I'll hurt myself. My dog died at the beginning of the year, right after the holidays. I was in shambles and couldn't stop the violent images blazing across my mind. Repeating routines with pathological slowness led to my losing my job in accounting. I was only there a year. It's been a while since I graduated from college, but as I said, when Charlie died, I couldn't come out of it on my own. They started me on an additional med to bolster fluoxetine. So far, I've only got anxiety and dizziness when I first stand up as side effects."

"Hi. My name is Stevie. Right now, I'm fifteen, but I'll be sixteen in July. I was just diagnosed this week with OCD. And I had my first therapy appointment, where she said that I could tell her anything, but what I said landed me in here, which isn't as bad as I'd imagined. The horrible images affected me as well. I'd see images of my family being hurt, so I was afraid to be around sharp things, and my therapist asked if I'd thought about harming anyone, and I'd said no. She asked numerous times, and each time I'd said no to her. Then the questions were changed up a little to something like 'Can you be certain that when you're angry with your little sister that you won't harm her?'" Stevie sniffles, "And I was uncertain with what she was asking and how I was supposed to respond, and then she left the room, and a large man, another therapist, guarded the door until the ambulance came. They gave me a shot that put me to sleep, and the medication I'm on made me sleepy at first, but it's not as powerful each time I take it.

And the other medicine doesn't work at all yet. That's why you see me tapping and counting again. I hope that I can go home on Monday."

Suddenly, there's a commotion in the hallway. Outside the glass window, somebody collapses, and the OCD group nurse leaves the group to offer her assistance. Other group therapy rooms let out as well. Nurses step out to see what's the matter and attempt to rein in the patients back into the therapy rooms until they get a wheelchair for the collapsed patient.

"It's time for the phones to open up. Everybody is anxious to get down to the bank of phones," Marvin says, tapping the table.

"Well, I guess that's the end of our group, too," Alice says. "It was nice meeting the new people. I hope that it was helpful for you, because I like this group and want people to keep coming back. I feel very comfortable with all of you. And it's good to hear that others experience similar things, and it's not just crazy me."

After the patient is transported down to her room, the groups are let out of their group therapy rooms. There is the hustle and bustle throughout the ward. Some people go for a snack; others form lines for the phones. Most take a restroom break and nap in their rooms. Stevie did a little of each.

"Mom, it's Stevie," Stevie calls home to the landline.

"Hi, sweetie. We're coming up to see you tonight." Morgan says.

"Good, I miss you guys," Stevia admits. "I'm sorry if I was a jerk last night and didn't hug you guys."

"Oh, darling, I love you," Liam says from another line in the house as well. "We'll be there for you."

Those words echo down the hallways and into her thoughts and dreams.

5 To Love a Shadow

By the time Morgan and Liam arrive, what was minutely working with her pills has worn off, and the rechecking, repeating, and asking that nothing terrible happened to her family ran amok. She tried napping but only dozes off for a few minutes, then bounces back up to alert status again.

"When will the doctor know it's time to change course and order up a different prescription?" Liam asks.

"Isn't this only the third day on this medication? The psychiatrist will probably want at least two weeks for good measure," one of the nurses tells Stevie and her parents.

"We love our daughter dearly, and it pains us to see her like this: a shadow of her former self," Liam wipes his eyes.

Not long after Liam and Morgan leave, it's time for Stevie's next dose of medicine. She takes it and nods off before it's time for lights out.

After a few awake times overnight, Stevie wakes to Molly crying.

"What's wrong?"

"Nothing, just go back to sleep," Molly whispers as she fiddles with something under her covers while tears stream down her face.

"What are you doing?" Stevie is curious and alarmed.

"Don't tell the nurses, okay?" Molly asks.

"Okay?" Stevie is hesitant.

"I found a safety pin on my former roommate's clothes holding her pairs of underwear together. The nurses probably didn't check so thoroughly for sharp objects on an OCD patient like they do for a self-injury person," Molly says, wavering between pain and euphoria.

"So, what are you doing with a safety pin? I mean, how are you self-harming? What does a safety pin do?" Stevie asks.

"I poke it into my skin."

"Like on your stomach?"

"More like my inner thighs, but high enough so if I'm made to wear shorts, nobody sees it."

"Does your mom make you wear shorts when you don't want to?" Stevie questions.

"I don't live with my mom anymore."

"And your dad?"

"He was sent to prison for abusing me. So he's out of the picture."

"Is your mom sick or something, where she can't take care of you?"

"Alcoholism is a sickness. But they took me away from her because she let my dad abuse me. That's why she lost custody and never bothered to try to get it back, so I'm in a group home," Molly informs.

"Is that foster care?" Stevie is curious.

"Yes and no. While I'm in the foster care system, I'm not with a foster care family at this time, thank god. I've heard scary stories. I'm in a home with seven other teens, and we have a caregiver, group home parent, at all times. There is always somebody who sleeps overnight, and a couple of others come in the morning to cook and drive us in a van to school. It's not that bad. It just kind of gets lonely when other girls form friendships, and you're left out in the cold; the rest of the people are best friends, and I'm the odd one out," Molly elaborates. Molly pulls the bloody safety pin out from under the sheets and uses the bathroom to dress.

Holy crap, what did I just see? Should I have told someone about it? Did she hurt herself? Am I a lousy friend for not getting help? Is this how Mom and Dad feel when I'm potentially hurting myself without the meds to keep me stable? What do I say to her when she comes out? Do I show interest and ask more questions? Or leave her alone with her secrets? I don't like being put in this situation. I wish that I hadn't seen what she was doing.

"Are you ready for breakfast?" Molly asks when she exits the bathroom.

"Just let me get dressed. If you want, I can meet you down there," Stevie says.

"No, I don't have any friends here either. Just acquaintances that have already found their best friends on the ward," Molly replies.

"Okay, just a second," Stevie uses the restroom and returns in jeans and a tee.

The two of them amble down to the dining commons and sit at a table with Jace and Cooper. When the rolling rack of food trays comes up, they take turns searching for their name on the nutrition card, which they'll use to order tomorrow's meal, should they still be there the next day.

"I hope that I won't be here tomorrow," Stevie says.

"You're tired of us already?" Jace jokes.

"Honestly, it's not as bad as I thought, but I miss my own bed, and my parents' rules aren't so demanding," Stevie replies.

"I was just kidding. I know you could never get tired of us," Jace nudges Cooper.

But Stevie sees behind them a couple of tables to where Elias sits. He was in her OCD group yesterday. He smiles at her. Just as she's ready to smile back, she notices the older guys, Marvin, Harvey, and Dennis, sitting next to him.

I don't want to let them see me smiling at Elias and make more out of it than there is. Is there any way? He's attractive in a shy sort of way. I wonder if he'll be at any of my groups today.

"What did you sign up for today?" Molly wonders.

"Horticulture therapy for a couple of hours this morning, lunch, then animal friends therapy for a couple of hours this afternoon, dinner, then group walk before my parents come to visit me," Stevie says.

"Exactly the same as me, but I won't be staying the full two hours in each. I have to attend self-injury group and sexual abuse survivors' group therapy," Molly whispers. Jace and Cooper are goofing around and don't listen to what Molly has to say anyway.

As breakfast ends and the patients stand in line to put their trays on the rolling cart of racks, Stevie and Elias back into each other. It surprises them both, and they're on alert, both having OCD.

"I'm sorry," Stevie says. "I'm usually more careful of personal space."

"Me, too. I'm sorry as well," Elias points his head in Jace's direction. "So, are you two together?"

"Oh, god, no, it was just an open table at breakfast. What about you? Are you with anyone?" Stevie asks.

"No," Elias whispers. "What groups are you going to today?"

"Horticultural therapy, animal therapy, and the group walk," Stevie says. "And you?"

"I'm late in signing up. I'll see what's open, and maybe I'll see you if that's okay with you?" Elias looks anywhere but at Stevie, but smiles when she nods her head and smiles back.

They part ways to their respective rooms. Stevie is elated, but she still does her sitting and standing ritual and taps her fingers on the side of the bed. Molly enters and looks perplexed.

"What were you and the new guy talking about at the tray rack?" Molly's attitude is off-putting.

"What's wrong?" Stevie inquires.

"Nothing. I just thought you and I were friends here. I never have friends anywhere that I get to do stuff with, and now you've got a boyfriend on the ward," Molly mumbles, then retreats to the bathroom. After about fifteen minutes, nurse Rebecca comes in to talk to Stevie.

"So, where's your roommate?" Rebecca wonders.

"In the bathroom," Stevie speeds up her tapping, and a tear streams down her face. She repeatedly stares at the bathroom door."

"Molly, you know the rules. Unlock the door," Rebecca stammers after trying the lock. She fans a set of keys and finds the correct one. "Molly, what's going on in here?"

Molly shakes her head.

"Answer me, Molly," Rebecca says, looking around the bathroom, then returning to a silent patient who has her lips pressed together.

Rebecca grabs hold of Molly and holds her head steady with her chin and, with one hand, pries apart Molly's lips and finds the large safety pin. Rebecca's taut and strong arms flick the pin out of Molly's mouth. Then the nurse lifts up Molly's shirt and pulls down her black yoga pants to find thin streaks of blood. Rebecca pulls the alarm to the nurse's station and presses the intercom, requesting a sedative for that room and the flailing Molly, who's now screaming.

After another large male nurse comes in and administers the shot, Molly gradually lessens her pinch on Rebecca's arm with one hand and pulls her hair with the other. Both nurses carry Molly to her bed.

"It's almost time for groups. I see you're signed up for three today. I'm very proud of you for moving slightly out of your comfort zone. Can I ask? How's it been going in here as roommates?"

"I thought it was going well, but all of a sudden, she asked who I was talking to at breakfast, then said she thought I was her friend in here. Then she rushed into the bathroom," Stevie informs.

"How long was she in there before I came in here?"

"Like fifteen minutes," Stevie shrugs and cries harder, "I didn't mean to upset her. I'm sorry. I was just talking to someone else for like a minute."

"Molly doesn't have much family as you do," Rebecca says.

"Yeah, she told me," Stevie interjects.

"So I think that she kind of latches on to people and places a burden upon their shoulders to be the perfect friend to replace that longing for someone who cares that family would normally offer."

"Okay, so I didn't do anything wrong?" Stevie asks, still tapping.

"No, you most certainly did not," Rebecca informs Stevie. "It's time to go down to the greenhouse in the courtyard. There are a couple of nurses who are also therapists in training who run the horticultural therapy group. I think five of you are signed up. Jonathan, the nurse who was just in here helping me with Molly, will be walking you guys down and waiting for you to finish."

"Hi, Stevie," Elias says as the group gathers near the locked entry doors to the unit while they wait for the nurse's station to unlock them.

The group takes the stairs down the four flights for some added exercise and continues the brief walk out into the courtyard. Once there, they sit around a table and make new plants from cuttings of mother plants, healthy houseplants. They then insert those little picks with balloons at the end that say things like "get well" and "thinking of you" to give to patients who don't have family, sending them flowers.

"Next, you're going to make living wreaths from overgrown pots of hens and chicks and other lush succulents from our greenhouse. You'll start with a wreath form and liner as well as floral pins, potting soil, and sand. The additional cactus and succulent cuttings of sedum, sempervivum, and echeveria plants in an assortment of sizes and colors will make the wreath dazzle with variety."

"What do we do first?" an older patient with early-onset dementia asks.

"You'll start by preparing the wreath form and arranging your liners inside. Watch me as I pack in a moist mixture of three parts potting soil to one part sand," the therapy nurse pauses to work with her wreath first. "Now, you guys will do it."

"I can't," the Parkinson's patient with anger management issues says. "My hands are shaking too much."

"I'll help you," offers a volunteer while the rest of the group works on their own. "And what is the sand used for?"

"It's for drainage for the plant," the therapy nurse directing them says. "Next, secure the wreath pieces together."

"What shall we do with the extra pieces of liner?" the volunteer asks.

"You can either cut it away or tuck it in the wreath," the facilitator says. "Then penetrate the liner with your pick while the wreath is lying flat on the table. Use your fingers to make small holes for each plant by pushing away the soil with the tips of your fingers." She models the example to them. "Then insert the plants into the openings and use the pins to secure them. Now just work your way around the wreath, doing the same thing each time. We'll be walking around the room to help each one of you individually as you work."

"I think that I've seen you in school before. Aren't you friends with Nico?" Elias says, be careful of his soil so that his spot remains orderly.

"Yes, I am," Stevie blushes while tapping her foot eight times, stopping, then starting again.

"You say you have OCD. I don't see you doing anything familiar."

"I do a lot of cleaning and organizing at all hours of the night. Some of my obsession revolves around food. It has to be cut into equal bites, or I'll choke. And I'm starting to eat less and less because the bite sizes are getting smaller, and my throat is constricting," Elias responds.

"When finished, these can either be used as wreaths or centerpieces," the facilitating nurse says as she stands between Elias and Stevie to help both of them move along and focus less on the dirt contamination. "It's okay to be messy with the dirt. We just sweep it up when we're done."

"That's easier said than done," Elias whispers to Stevie.

Afterward, for hour two, which only Stevie and Elias stay for, the volunteer staffers bring in bags and boxes of supplies to make faux summer centerpieces. There are baskets, foam core, floral pins, fake grass, moss, lichens, flowers, pine cones, acorns, butterflies, dragonflies, ribbon, and other tiny odds and ends to decorate the pieces.

"That is so excellent. In the span of an hour, you each made four faux centerpieces. Just think of the smiles your work will bring to the faces of the recipient patients who wouldn't otherwise receive a get-well gift. Job well done, Stevie and Elias."

On the way back up the stairs to the ward, they walk together behind the male psych nurse. They take turns glancing at each other and smiling. Once they're back on the ward, they stand together by the phone bank, looking a little bit uncomfortable.

"It's still a half-hour until lunch. Do you want

to play a game of checkers or something?" Elias asks.

"Sure," Stevie responds and follows him to the board game cart at the far edge of the dining room.

As they set up the board and make it orderly, Elias asks, "Do you think I can get your number to text you sometimes?"

"Sure, I'll write it down the next time I go to my room," Stevie replies.

After they play two quick games, the cart of lunch trays is wheeled in, and they clean up, then get their lunches and sit together quietly until Marvin and Lucy join them. The latter two carry on the conversation at the table through lunch and cleanup, then the four part ways. Elias and Stevie each return to their separate rooms.

Stevie finds a nurse sitting with a groggy Molly on her roommate's side of the room.

"I'm sorry that I blew up at you, Stevie," Molly says.

"That's okay," Stevie pulls out her journal and writes her name and cell phone number on the top corner of a page. When the nurse leaves, she tears it out and puts it in her pocket, then returns to the torn page left inside the journal and methodically resumes pulling out the saw-toothed remnants of the page, so the journal pages once again have clean lines. "Will you be joining us in the gym for the animal therapy at 1:00 pm?

"I can't since I've lost my privileges for the rest of today for the stint that I pulled this morning and for yelling at you," Molly says, wiping tears from her eyes.

When it's time for the pet therapy session,

nearly half of the ward's thirty patients stand and line up to unlock the doors to the gymnasium and take floor pillows to sit at an equal distance apart. With the exception of Molly, all of the ward's teens attend. In addition, all of the OCD group is in attendance. Stevie taps the floor repeatedly while Elias resets his pillow so it isn't crooked against the linoleum tile. Henry and Lucy sit and stand over and over again, while Marvin counts and blinks numerous times before he can sit down. Once Elias is seated, he clears his throat fifteen times. When the three dogs are brought in, they meander around the patients, patiently waiting for their turns.

Time goes by quickly when playing the canines, and it is a resounding success with the OCD patients that, for the most part, forget about their obsessions, if only for a brief time. One by one, people leave, especially after 2:00 pm when the phone bank opens up. Elias and Stevie are the last in the room to play with the perky pets.

"Gross. I'm going to need to wash my hands and face after this," Stevie says.

"All the way up my arms, too," giggles Elias in agreement.

At 2:30, Stevie and Elias leave the pets to their owners, wash up, and then go to get in line for the phone bank.

"Mom, how are you doing?" Stevie asks. "Are you coming up at 3:00 pm or 7:00 pm?"

"We were thinking at 3:00. So we'll see you shortly. We're leaving right now, sweetie."

A few minutes after 3:00 pm, Stevie watches her parents go through an inspection at the nurse's station. Then Stevie runs up and hugs Dad first and then Mom. She takes her parents into the dining area and sits a few tables over from Elias and his parents.

"So, how's it going? Have you made any hospital friends? Where's your roommate?" Mom asks.

"She lost her privileges, so she can't come out for visiting hours and can't use the phones, yet," Stevie says.

"Why did she get her privileges suspended? Did she act out? Were you hurt?" Mom speaks a little too loudly, and the rest of the family looks in their direction.

"No, I wasn't hurt, Mom. Shh. Molly hurt herself, and the nurses caught her with a safety pin," Stevie whispers.

"Oh, well, that's all. What harm can one do with a safety pin?" Mom still speaks loud enough that others can hear her.

Stevie gestures to lower her voice. "Molly drew blood, and yes, you can do harm with the larger size safety pins. I guess anything sharp is dangerous," Stevie whispers again.

"Have you attended the weekend therapy groups?" Dad asks.

Stevie goes on to tell them about her group sessions and therapy off the ward. Every once in a while, she and Elias glance in one another's direction. So much so that both Elias's dad and Stevie's dad nod a greeting to each other. The mothers are so focused on inspecting their teenage children for injury and signs of well-being.

6 The Lives of Lies

"Do you know that boy over there?" Dad asks.

"Ah, yeah, he's in one of my groups. Why do you ask?"

"No reason, I guess. I just thought I noticed him looking over in this direction a few times," Liam responds.

"Oh, she'd never be interested in anyone from here," Mom interjects. You're just a hypervigilant dad, Liam."

"No, he's cool. You'd like him, Dad?" Stevie replies.

"What is he in here for?" Liam wonders.

"Same as me, with OCD," Stevie says.

"He looks a little older than you, Stevie."

"Just over a year, that's all."

"What are you guys wasting time talking about other patients for? Stevie will be out of here soon. She'll never see any of these people again, right Stevie?" Mom asks.

"No, I guess not," Stevie responds, glancing at Elias when her dad looks away. Stevie begins tapping on the table.

"So, last night, you mentioned pet therapy and horticultural therapy. Did you attend either one? What were they like?"

"Oh, Mom, it was so much fun. There was a golden lab, a dalmatian, and a silver-gray dog. I can't remember what they were called, though."

"Weimaraner?" Dad wonders.

"Yeah, that sounds like what the owner called it," Stevie replies.

"Did the dog calm you? I guess I mean did it

stop your obsessions and compulsions?"

"It did. The nurses even said so," Stevie says.

"How long did you get to interact with the dogs?" Dad asks.

"Over an hour," Stevie replies. "Before that, in horticulture therapy, we made faux centerpieces and a living wreath as gifts to the patients in the hospital who don't have families to give them gifts."

"How considerate a thing to do." Mom adds.

"Do you know what's going to happen tomorrow? Will I be released?" Stevie questions.

"We sure hope so," Dad adds, "I think it depends on your behavior here in this medical unit."

"You can call it a psych ward, Dad. It is what it is."

"I think that I've been doing everything that they tell me."

"Then let us all just hope for the best," Mom says.
I will be here as soon as they give us the green light."

After chatting over daily happenings at home and Piper's up-to-the-minute goings-on, they bid their goodbyes at the same time as Elias's parents, ready to leave.

Elias says, "How'd that go for you?"

"Good, and you?" Stevie questions.

"Pretty good; I'm going to take a short nap. I'll see you at dinner," Elias smiles.

Stevie nods her head and blushes, and then each returns to their respective rooms. When Stevie reaches her room, she finds the nurse at Molly's bed again. Stevie tries to enter quietly, but both look in her direction.

"How's it going out there today?" Molly asks.

"Good. How are you doing?"

"Do you still have a boyfriend?" Molly prods.

"I don't have a boyfriend. Elias and I are just friends."

"Did you attend plant and pet therapy together?"

"Yes, but I attended with other people as well. Are you going to ask if Lucy and I are an item?"

The nurse nudges Molly, who says, "I'm sorry. Do you want to sit together at dinner?"

"Um, yes, sure," Stevie says, which makes both Molly and the nurse happy.

Molly keeps an eager eye on Elias at dinner as he stands in line for his meal tray. Molly grabs her tray before Elias and turns to sit next to Lucy and Marvin. When Stevie gets her tray next, she is bewildered as to what to do.

"Stevie, I'm right here," Molly raises her voice, and the entire room looks at them.

Elias takes a spot at an empty table, and Stevie goes to sit by Molly. Stevie's back to back with Elias, who stands and repeatedly sits, eating only a handful of bites from his tray, returning it to the cart, and leaving the dining room.

Stevie ends up walking along with the older patients from the ward and between the two nurses. Elias never showed up for the walk, and Molly still didn't have privileges to attend. Stevie returns in tears to her room, where Molly tries to pick up a conversation, but Stevie is reserved and quietly readies for a shower and then proceeds to comb her hair repeatedly, trying to get the strands in the formation that she desires. Stevie willingly takes her meds when dispensed, but Molly resists and fights. A pair of nurses carries her off to a solitary room for reflection.

"What happened to Molly?" Stevie asks psych nurse Rebecca the first thing the next morning.

Rebecca takes a seat in the only chair in the room that Stevie shares with Molly. "Molly's been here the longest on the ward. When she meets somebody that she gets along well with, like you, she may act up a little bit when she knows you're leaving."

"Am I leaving?" Stevie is giddy.

"Here's your pills. That's the recommendation from us nurses. We'll have to see how your appointment with the psychiatrist goes, though. He may deem a few more days are necessary to see how the meds are working before he discharges you."

"If I do leave, will I get to say goodbye to Molly?" Stevie asks.

"That probably won't be such a good idea."

"Why don't you get dressed and come out for breakfast? Then we'll put you in line to see the doctor, okay?" Rebecca says.

As Stevie walks around the corner, she sees Elias and gets excited, but he doesn't look her way. Instead, he goes to sit with the guys at a different table. Stevie plans her bites accordingly to be finished at the same time as Elias so she can talk to him, but he rushes past her and out of the dining area and down the hall to his room. She's deflated, so she returns to her room until she's called for the appointment with the psychiatrist first thing.

"How are you doing, Stevie?"

"I think that I'm much better. I'm getting used

to the side effects of the pills, but I don't think they help as much as they're supposed to?"

The psychiatrist reads over his paperwork, "So you've joined in on the groups here?"

"Yes, being up here wasn't as bad as I thought it would be."

"There was an issue with your roommate?"

"I don't know what that was about, honestly," Stevie replies.

"Yes, I see. That's what it says here. She grew attached to you?"

"I think so."

"So, how are the obsessive thoughts?" the psychiatrist asks.

"The same, but I don't plan on acting on them," Stevie promises.

"And if I release you today, do you plan on returning to see your psychiatrist and therapist as planned?"

"Yes, yes, I will."

"And you'll be open and honest with them?"

"Yes."

"And you'll keep up with your medication?"

"Absolutely."

"And cognitive behavioral therapy?"

"I will."

"Then, by all accounts, I don't see any reason for you to stay any longer. The nurses will notify your parents that they can pick you up immediately. Try to get in to see your therapist at least today or tomorrow. Goodbye, Ms. Mathews."

"Goodbye," Stevie is overjoyed.

Once in the hall, she bumps into someone and turns around, and finds out it's Elias.

"I'm sorry, Elias," Stevie shouts.

"That's okay, Stevie. I'm fine." Elias responds while backing away to be alongside Marvin.

What the hell did I do to him? Why the sudden change in behavior? Is this just from dinner last night? I had to sit with Molly, or she would've made a scene. What am I thinking? He probably just never really liked me. Why was I guessing a guy could be interested in me? After all, we just went to a couple of therapy groups that were practically mandatory because we were expected to interact with each other. That's what it was, mandatory group interaction. He was just cordial, and I took it as more. I am so stupid. What should I do now? Go back to my room and wait alone? Well, I can't exactly go to touch base group if I'm leaving within the hour? Damn. I really liked him.

"Stevie, I will call your mom and be right down to discharge you. Wait in your room," Rebecca says rather loudly.

"Congratulations, Stevie," Lucy says. "Hey, I know that I'm twenty-two, and you're like fifteen, but do you want to exchange texts on our OCD journeys?

"That'd be great," Stevie says. "Let me get you my number." Stevie writes on

"Hey, by the way, I think Elias likes you," Lucy adds. "He was asking Marvin what he thought about you."

"Really," Stevie is surprised.

"He's really cute, don't you think?" Lucy wonders.

"Yeah, I think so."

"Stevie, are you ready?" Rebecca interrupts and waits. "So how do you feel now that you know you'll be leaving us?"

"I'm well. I don't think the medication is working like it's supposed to, but I don't feel suicidal or like I'll harm anybody if that's what you're asking."

"You're definitely going to be discharged. I was just wondering your feelings about your stay and impending departure?"

"It wasn't as bad as I'd thought. I liked the group therapies. And the people were really nice," Stevie admits, sitting and standing eight times.

"We worked with your mom's schedule and made two appointments for you tomorrow with both your psychiatrist and your therapist," Rebecca says.

"Yay," Stevie is sarcastic.

"If you want to pack up your clothes, your mom will be here at the top of the hour." Rebecca leaves the room.

Once out of the ward, down the stairs, and into the car, Mom says, "I just stopped by your school to pick up the last of your textbooks. Apparently, your instructors sent all the assignments by email. When you return on Wednesday, you'll make up tests in the library with the proctor."

Stevie rushes to her basement bedroom at home and fires up her laptop to find the latest emails from her best friends since her phone has to charge up.

To: Stevie Mathews

From: Nicolas Montgomery
CC: Isadora Madsen
Subject: hospital stay

What happened to you? I'm in Bio again, and we're supposed to be doing some online worksheets, but I'm too focused on what's going on with you, Stevie. You'd better make it back in time to dissect the baby pig for finals. I don't want to have to find a different partner.

Stevie rushes through the plethora of emails from her teachers with instructions on worksheets and reading assignments. And more English vocabulary self-quizzes and another Spanish grammar packet. Finally, the email she's been looking for the past five minutes.

To: Stevie Mathews
From: Isadora Madsen
CC: Nicolas Montgomery
Subject: Re: hospital stay

Did you see anybody from school in the psych ward? What was it like? I imagine howling screams from solitary confinement throughout the night. Any fights? Were you scared to fall asleep with your roommate six feet from where you slept?

Stevie pulls the bedspread off her bed and remakes it to her stringent standards. She reorganizes the perfume bottles on her dresser, then rearranges the makeup on her vanity table near the window.

To: Isadora Madsen
From: Stevie Mathews
CC: Nicolas Montgomery
Subject: Re: hospital stay

I found out that I don't have to attend summer school if I can complete all my backed-up school work. I have some tests with the library proctor set for the day I return, which is Wednesday. I'm waiting for my phone to charge up and see if you sent me any texts. I hope you did. I missed you guys.

"Stevie, I'm going to the grocery store again. Do you want to get out in the fresh air and come along? What would you like for dinner?"

Stevie runs upstairs, then back to the bottom step, and leads with the correct foot this time. Once at the top landing, Stevie sees disaster. It's a new rug, and it has fringes.

"Mom, I can't do it," Stevie cries. "That's my worst nightmare."

"Can't do what?" Mom asks. "Stevie, what's wrong?"

"The fringes are making me flip out. I can't be in the same room with them," Stevie bawls. "Mom, you need to get rid of that rug."

"Okay, honey, but it's a rather large piece of carpet, plus the furniture is too heavy to move by myself. I'll need to wait for your dad to help me." Mom says.

"Well, let's get out for a little bit and get the

groceries for dinner," Mom says. "And we can stop and get some lunch."

"Okay, I need to leave now, though," Stevie slips on her shoes and strokes the feng shui coins on the front entry door trim with the back of her fingers eight times.

Stevie rushes out to the SUV and waits for Mom to bring the keys. Stevie takes the lint roller from the console to clean the driver's seat thoroughly when she does. Mom is massaging her temples.

"Stevie, maybe it might be best if you stay home this time."

"I can't be in the same house with that rug," Stevie says, arranging the pens in the cup holder correctly: blue, purple, then red.

While she backs out of the driveway, the pens jostle, and Stevie has to fix them before she starts down the moderately busy residential street that's a cut across between the highway and the high school. As she moves down the street, the pens shake up again. She reaches to reorder them.

"Stevie," Morgan screams.

"What, Mom?" Stevie is too late to stop from rear-ending a little import station wagon.

After Morgan and the other driver finish exchanging Stevie's and the other woman's license and insurance information, plus taking pics of the vehicles, Stevie starts to drive again. That's only after Mom puts the pens in her purse.

"Five, six, seven, no," Stevie says and rounds the corner.

"What are you doing, Stevie? What's going on now?"

"I was taught that when I'm having obsessive thoughts to count all the blue things in the room. Any color actually but to start counting because it uses a different side of the brain," Stevie informs.

"That doesn't make sense because now you're compulsively counting something else," Morgan says.

"No, I'm doing it wrong. I was supposed to be focused on the color, not the amount or something. Anyway, I'm stuck now. I have to end on a good number, and there were thirteen shades of blue cars on that street."

"Oh, no, Stevie," Mom replies. "We can't keep doing this."

"I know, Mom. I realize that it doesn't make sense, but if I don't do it, something bad will happen."

"No, Stevie. It won't. I promise you. Just stop. Please, for me."

"I can't, Mom. Just one more time. Maybe there is a good number of white cars," Stevie says as she turns the corner.

To cut the counting to the right number, they turn in the post office, and Morgan runs inside for stamps while Stevie waits in the car, crying. When Morgan exits, a number of people are talking to Stevie, asking her if she's okay.

"Is this your mom?"

"Why is she crying?"

"My daughter is fine. Please leave us alone."

"She is grief-stricken. What happened to her?" an elderly woman wonders.

"She's fine. We need to go now."

"What did you do to her to make her cry like

that?" an older man asks.

"Get out of our way," Morgan yells.

"No, I'm calling the police. She shouldn't be crying like that," the elderly woman says.

"Oh, god damn it. My daughter has a mental illness. I just picked her up from the psych ward. Mind your own god damn business and leave us alone," Morgan yells.

The group backed off. They keep staring at Stevie, but she's unaware of anyone around her. Morgan goes to the driver's side and tells Stevie to climb over the seat into the passenger's side. She does. Morgan takes the wheel and squeals out of the parking lot.

7 True Hearts and False Faces

"Mom, I can't go in that house with that rug in there?" Stevie proclaims.

"Honey, I can't move the rung by myself. It's too heavy. And you need to lie down. If that display at the post office was any indication, I think that you need your medicine and to rest," Mom says.

"I'll sleep out here in the SUV."

"No, you won't."

"It'll be okay. I'll have the windows down," Stevie says.

"Come inside the garage door and through the mudroom. Don't even look towards the living room," Mom suggests.

"Okay, but if this doesn't work, just remember that I told you so," Stevie reminds.

"It will be my fault. I'll take the blame. Just come in."

May 22nd, 1:45 pm
Basement Bedroom
Dear Journal,

Life sucks. There's no other way to put it. I can't go on living like this. And I can't tell my therapist that because she'll have me locked up again. But being out of the hospital brings back everything tenfold. I mean, for some reason, it felt okay to be nuts in the psych ward. I didn't worry about my obsessions and compulsions because other people had them, too. Now that I'm home, everything is flaming before my eyes. I feel out of control, apart from my body.

Maybe it was too soon to leave. Should I have stayed in the hospital? I've only been on medication for five days. Not only do we not know if it is working, but do we even know that it's the correct diagnosis? I mean, really. I'm not far off from that guy with paranoid schizophrenia. I mean, I have these thoughts telling me to do things like straightening the fringes. Bad things will happen. And my family will die. At least the guy with the paranoia is getting the right medication.

And, oh no, what about school on Wednesday? What if I flip out in the testing center in the library? Everyone will know how much of a freak I really am for the next three years until I graduate. It's just like the damn therapist with the well-meaning heart, as Mom calls it, but her face tells the real story. One wrong word and I'm back at the hospital.

"Mom, are you up here?" Stevie says at the main floor landing, where she peers into the kitchen.

A heaviness sets in her chest, more like a tightness and a lightness in her head. She walks around the corner to the living room, where the rug lies adversarial, almost beckoning the fight. She thinks of her dad on his commute home from work across the bridge. What if it collapses? She can't let that happen. Stevie falls to the floor and arranges the fringes equidistant and taut.

"Stevie," Mom yells as she descends the stairs to find her daughter lying on the floor. Once she realizes what Stevie's doing, Mom doesn't know whether to worry less or more. "You have to get up. This is irrational. Why hasn't the damn medicine started working yet? I thought you'd come home better than when you went in. Shit."

Mom picks up the phone, "Liam, Stevie's on the floor." Morgan pauses. "No, she's having a fit over the rug. You've got to get home. I can't deal with this crap right now. I've got a business dinner tonight for the Murphy project. We're pitching over dinner, and I need to get ready, and this is making me want to pull my own hair out. Come home now."

Almost an hour later, Mom is dressed and by the desk in the living room, working on her tablet when Liam and Piper enter the front door to find Stevie still on the wood floor, straightening the ends of the carpet fringes.

"Stevie, are you okay?" Piper asks, spurting tears at the sight of her hyper-agitated older sister.

"She's going to be fine, sweetie," Dad assures.

"Why don't you go get a snack, then go down to your room to do homework?"

"Are you going to take Stevie back to that hospital?" Piper wonders.

"No. Obviously, they didn't help her," Morgan snaps.

"What do we do then?" Liam asks.

"She meets with the shrink and therapist again tomorrow. They've got to come up with something. Nobody should have to live like this," Morgan responds.

"Are you okay?" Liam questions.

"Stevie flipped out on the way to the grocery store. Sorry, never made it to pick up supplies. We detoured to the much closer post office, but to our surprise. She flipped out there, too. Passersby thought I was abusing her or something to make her cry like she was. I ended up blowing up at them and telling everybody that I just picked her up from the psych ward. I don't know. Maybe it was better when she was in there," Morgan elaborates.

"Don't say that," Liam asserts, "She's our daughter, and we want her here safe with us."

"Then you work from home, too. At least while she's acting up, I can't do this alone. I work, too."

"I know you do. Has she taken her medicine? It knocked her out that first night."

"Her body is growing used to it," Mom replies.

"Well, it's not working," Liam sits on the floor next to Stevie.

"Tomorrow, they're just going to tell us to wait out the two weeks to see if it kicks in," Mom responds. Then she mumbles, "I never would've imagined where it would get this bad that I'd think she was better off there than with us."

"Don't say that," Liam orders.

"She's in pain, mental anguish," Mom says.

"Well, if she were in the hospital, she'd be the same way," Liam counters.

"No, she wouldn't because they'd have a sedative they'd be able to use. We don't have access to that here."

"This is going to be a long night," Liam predicts. "I gave her the evening medicine, but there's been no difference."

"You're coming with us tomorrow for that shrink appt," Mom demands before she leaves for her dinner meeting, tablet in hand.

Six hours and a plethora of tears later, Mom returns home from her business meeting, overworked and undernourished. Her yawning comes to an abrupt end once she sees her eldest daughter crouching in the corner, crying. Dad holds Stevie's hands and pleads with her to give up the relentless pursuit of perfection.

"That's it. Let's get rid of this rug. Help me move the furniture off of it, Morgan, please?" Liam instructs.

"Has she been at this all evening?" Morgan asks.

"Yes, and I don't see it ending tonight unless we get rid of this rug."

"What are we going to do with it this late? If we put it out in the garage, she'll be out there all night. Tell me that you recognize that, Liam."

"I'm not going to be able to sleep knowing she's in such pain over this damn thing. We'll put it in the back of my truck, and I'll haul it to a dumpster somewhere."

After moving the rug out to Dad's truck, Stevie settles down a bit. Mom rushes up to shower and change, and when she returns, Stevie is in the same spot she left her. She takes Stevie by the hand and leads her down to her basement bedroom, and helps her into the shower while she finds clothes, making sure to touch as little as possible. When Stevie exits the bathroom, she is brushing her hair in a precise fashion.

"I guess there's no telling you that it's illogical; whatever you're thinking will happen if you don't attend to such detail with your hair," Mom says when Dad knocks and enters the room.

"Where did you take the rug?"

"The sign at the thrift store read no dumping, but it's a brand new rug that we shelled out $800 or more for, so I wasn't about to just destroy it. Someone will put it to good use," Liam says.

"Well, we should probably go to bed and try to get some sleep," Morgan suggests.

"You go ahead. I'll sleep on the sofa in the family room so I can hear if she gets up in the middle of the night and tries to leave or anything like that," Liam replies.

"I don't think that's necessary," Morgan counters.

"Given what's happened today, you can assure me that the night will be nothing out of the ordinary?" Liam poses.

"I'll get some sheets and make up the sofa in there," Morgan responds.

After a relatively uneventful night of Stevie

moving things around in her room at all hours of the night, but all the while staying stable, Morgan wakes Stevie and Liam for breakfast.

"Stevie, you rearranged your room," Morgan states.

"I couldn't sleep. And something just looked lopsided. I couldn't place it, but now it's better," Stevie replies.

"And you braided your hair?" Liam notes.

"I couldn't get it to sit right. This was the only option," Stevie says with a lint roller in hand. "My clothes are all full of lint. Where is Charlie anyway?"

"Probably with Piper, like usual," Liam responds.

At breakfast, Stevie takes juice in tiny pours that amount to eight. She cuts her sausage into eight pieces and rearranges her scrambled eggs so that they're in eight distinct little piles on her plate, none of which are touching. Every time she uses her stylus to make a note on her tablet, she carefully washes it with a baby wipe.

"Breakfast went off without a hitch," Liam says, packing his satchel for work. "I will be at the doctors' with you two, but I do have to run into work for a couple of hours today. I'm sorry, but I have to do it. It's my job, hon," Liam pleads.

"If that's all I can get out of you today, then I'll take it, but we need to press for more action. We can't continue to live like this, Liam."

After dropping Piper off at school, Liam meets up in the parking lot of the counseling center. "So, where do we go from here?"

Stevie leads the way, "Follow me, Dad."

Inside at the elevator, the line is rather long, so

they wait until the next one. Liam stays by Stevie's side as she checks in for the psychiatrist appointment first. When Dr. Williams calls them, he's a little bit surprised that Dad joins them.

"Dads don't usually join unless something is going very wrong," Dr. Williams states.

"We can't continue to live like this. It's physically separating us and mentally pounding at us from all angles. Who knows what will set it off the next time?" Morgan cries.

"We need to give the medicine time to work. It's only been six days since her first dose," Dr. Williams suggests.

"We have jobs. We need our sleep. That can't happen if we have to be up watching and listening for her every move. Even beyond all of that stuff, Stevie is in pain, mentally."

"What happened?" Dr. Williams inquires.

"Physically collapsing on the floor to fix the fringes on a rug for hours on end until we finally had to lug it out and dispose of it in the middle of the night," Liam elaborates.

"She was devastated. Physically and emotionally, from the stupid area rug," Morgan adds. "We couldn't just leave her alone in pain. We took turns staying with her, but we both have jobs. Plus, Stevie herself has school. How can we send her back like this?"

"As far as school goes, I'll have my assistant write something up for disability services at the high school. Stevie will get the opportunity to make up her work as soon as she feels better," Dr. Williams promises.

"There's got to be something else we can be

doing," Liam presses.

"We'll try a sedative in addition to the antidepressant and mood stabilizer, but I don't want Stevie in control of her meds. One of you two needs to dispense this benzodiazepine up to three times daily as needed. The sedating effect should last four to six hours. It most likely will make her sleepy but calm. It was used on Stevie in the hospital," Dr. Williams informs.

"Why are we just hearing about this now?" Liam demands.

"It's highly addictive. We don't like prescribing it as a first option, but in this instance, it might be necessary."

"Something's necessary because we are at our wits' end," Liam slaps his hands on his knees, then leans back in the office chair and struggles to sigh.

"I'll want to continue the therapy with Shelby three times a week, especially while we are using this added medication."

"Is she supposed to return to school while she's on the sedative?" Liam asks.

"It all depends on how her body reacts to it," Dr. Williams replies. "I know it's difficult, but we need to take it one day at a time. Shelby will be of great help during this time. If there isn't anything else, I can show you down to her office."

"No, thank you for your time. When do we see you again?" Liam wonders.

"Next week," Dr. Williams stands to guide them, "I'm so sorry for all your troubles. Trust that all that is possible is being done. It just takes some time."

"Forgive me for my tone," Liam says. "We are just at our limits as to what we can do for her, and it's difficult relying on an outsider to make our family right again."

"Well, you're in good hands with Shelby," Dr. Williams says as he knocks on the door. "Shelby, are you ready for the Mathews family? Dad is joining them today."

"Welcome, please take a seat. Thank you, Dr. Williams."

"Hello, I'm Liam Mathews, Stevie's dad."

"Nice to meet you. And it's good to see you again, Mrs. Mathews and Stevie?"

"I'm afraid to talk to you. I realize that you may have a true heart, but your face tells lies."

"Stevie," Mom spurts.

"It's okay, Morgan. I want Stevie to be honest with me. We won't get anywhere unless we're honest." Shelby ascertains.

"I didn't appreciate being sideswiped from out of nowhere.".

"Please realize that I did what I had to do, Stevie," Shelby swears. "It was in the best interest of your entire family. You want your little sister to be safe, don't you?"

"Well, yes, but you twisted my words. You gave me false intentions. You were two-faced."

"Can we just agree to start over?" Shelby pleads.

"If you're not going to twist my thoughts," Stevie crosses her arms across her chest.

"My intentions were pure. Let's begin again—"

8 My Dreams of You Will Stay

"Stevie, you need to take this right now," Morgan says, holding a water bottle and Stevie's prescriptions.

Stevie is in her basement bedroom, rearranging her bed, dresser, vanity, bookcase, and desk.

"I can't come up until I'm finished."

"Then, I'll come down there," Mom yells until she opens the door and hands Stevie the water bottle, and doles out a pill. "I'll be checking on you again in half an hour."

Just then, a text comes in:

Elias: Hey Stevie. It's Elias. I just got released.
Elias: I didn't know if U wanted to talk to me.
Elias: U kind of blew me off at dinner.
Stevie: My roommate was jealous of U
Elias: Oh. How R things now?
Stevie: So UR out?
Elias: R U back at school?
Stevie: Not for a few days.
Elias: What's up?
Stevie: I had an episode with a fringe carpet.
Elias: That must've been hell.
Stevie: It sucks.
Elias: Same meds?
Stevie: He added a sedative.
Elias: Those R always good.
Stevie: I'm rearranging my room.
Elias: I'm making a list of things to do.
Stevie: I should be doing homework.
Elias: I'll get to mine soon.
Stevie: I'm sorry I ignored U.

Elias: I'm sorry I walked away.
Stevie: We're cool.
Elias: So, do U want to get a frappé?
Stevie: When?
Elias: I can pick U up b4 school?
Elias: Or take U home after?
Stevie: After is better when I get back
Elias: Sounds great.
Stevie: It's making me sleepy.
Elias: OK, catch U later
Stevie: Bye

"Stevie, how are you doing?" Mom opens the door and finds Stevie just sitting on her bed in a daze.

"Okay."

"Why don't you lie down before you fall down, sweetie. Please," Mom begs.

"I need my journal tablet on my desk," Stevie stammers.

"I'll get it for you," Mom says. "I'll set it right here. Just close your eyes and relax." Mom pulls the throw over Stevie. "I love you, baby."

May 23rd, 5:33 pm

Basement Bedroom

Dear Journal,

I've slept off most of the day. It isn't easy remembering what I was doing before the last dose of medication. Wait.

I had a text conversation with Elias. That's a breakthrough. Yes. I think he might like me. Oh, god. I hope Lucy at the hospital didn't tell him that I thought he was cute. I'd just die. I'll have to ask her. Where's her number? My thoughts are rogue:

- Well, this sedative takes the edge off my obsessions and compulsions, but will I be able to stay awake in school?

- What is my going to be like? Will I always be on medication?

- Or will I get used to it like the other medicines that wore off after a few doses, granted they were low doses, Dr. Williams said.

- And how do I tell my mom and dad about Elias taking me out for coffee drinks?

- I lied to them. Will they forgive me?

- Will they give Elias a chance?

- Should I be giving Elias a chance? I hardly know him. He might be violent. No. He's too laid back. But how do I know for sure? Nico?

"Stevie, are you awake? I thought I heard your bathroom door close. If so, come up and get some dinner?"

"Mom, I'm up. Are Dad and Piper home yet?"

"He's up changing, and Piper is finishing some homework. So how do you think the medicine worked?"

"I'm still obsessed and have compulsions, but the need to act on every single one is sort of clouded by my being sleepy or dazed, something like that. It's difficult to explain."

"I think that you're doing an excellent job of explaining. I kind of get how you feel, sweetie," Mom says.

"Good," Stevie washes and scrubs her hands eight times in the powder room off the mudroom. "Can I help set the table?"

"Oh, Stevie, that's not necessary. I'll do it," Mom worries.

"You think I'll flip out again, don't you?" Stevie counters.

"Go ahead and set the table," Mom caves.

"Hey, Dad. I can't hug you right now since I just cleaned up. Mom said I could set the table."

"I see that," Dad gives Mom a weighty glance that spills a heft of emotion for everyone to see.

"Hey, Piper," Stevie says. "Am I missing much in school?"

"Not in my school. I bet yours is so much better," Piper replies.

"Why is that?"

"You get to have boyfriends and do whatever you want. We have to study the things they tell us, and boys my age are so childish," Piper tells Stevie, who is only a quarter of the way finished with setting the placemats and dinnerware.

"Oh, Piper, sweetie. I don't think Stevie is thinking about boys right now. She's got so much more important things to focus on at the moment," Mom says.

"Actually, about that. Can I leave for school early on Thursday? I'll be picked up. We're going to the coffee shop and then straight to school."

"With whom?" Dad interjects.

"A new friend," Stevie is coy.

"How have you made any new friends. The only places you been for the last week and a half are here and the hospital," Dad prods.

"Oh, no, sweetie. Did you meet somebody at the hospital? That can't be a good thing, Liam?" Mom fears.

"Is it that boy from the dining room that you said that you didn't know?" Dad jabs. "You lied to us? That isn't the way that you get privileges in this house."

"Stevie, no one from that psych ward, please?" Mom begs.

"He's actually a friend of Nico's." Stevie snaps. "A friend just like me that ended up in the psych ward to get adjusted to medicine that is being used on us like guinea pigs. Why let's try this dose of this one and add a little of that for fun? You don't realize how heavy this weight is that I'm carrying. Can't I just go for a frappé? I'm not asking to marry him."

"Watch your tone, Stevie," Dad warns. "Perhaps this once, but I want to meet him before he takes you? Is it him or his mom driving?"

"He's got his own car?" Stevie bristles with

anticipation at the next question.

"So, he's sixteen?" Mom spurts.

"Seventeen." Stevie stands still and closes her eyes.

"Now, wait a minute. If he's seventeen at the end of this school year, next school year he must be—"

"A senior?" Mom finishes Dad's sentence.

"That means he'll be turning eighteen. No way, Stevie," Dad sets his foot down.

"Stevie—"

"You're five years older than Mom. I can't believe this. Hypocrites. I've lost my appetite." Stevie rushes out of the room and down the stairs.

Stevie bounds into her room and slams the door, immediately regretting one she didn't finish setting the table to her specs and secondly that she didn't get something to eat because she's starving. Stevie digs in her backpacks for a bar, a bag of chips, anything, but there isn't a crumb. She's too tidy for that scenario.

"Stevie," Mom says through the locked door. "You need to eat something."

Stevie can't hear her because of the earbuds and through sheer obstinance, so she sketches and thinks:

If I don't stand my ground now, will I ever get a boyfriend? For Chrissakes, Dad had already started working on his Master's Degree when Mom started as a Freshman at the U. This is nothing but crap. Maybe Nico can help. What do I say? Do you know a guy named Elias? I think I'm in love with him.

He's so good-looking and sweet, not like any of the typically arrogant and ignorant juniors and seniors.

She looks at her phone, and nothing. Where the hell are her best friends? Did they ditch her and start doing stuff with someone else?

To: Stevie Mathews
From: Nicolas Montgomery
CC: Isadora Madsen
Subject: status?

What happened to you? Your mom answered the door and said that you were napping and it was best to let you get caught up on some sleep. Shit. Girl. Are you down for the count? We're working on the study packets for bovine dissection. You're still my partner, right? Text me when you can. Or email. I'm here. Love you, buddy!

Stevie rushes through an onslaught of emails from her teachers, the school nurse, the principal, and now the school counselor.

To: Stevie Mathews
From: Isadora Madsen
CC: Nicolas Montgomery
Subject: Re: status?

Your mom also said that she didn't want us to be texting you to wake you up. How long are you going to sleep? I mean. Shit. What are they giving you? Are you okay? I'm serious now. You hear stories about kids messed with by doctors or parents. I don't want to think that about old Liam and Morgan, but they're keeping you from us under the guise of your safety. Hey, BFF, don't you forget about me, okay?

Stevie stomps her feet on the floor from where she sits. She leans forward and pulls out a gob of hair. When she lifts her head up, she wipes the tears from her eyes and focuses her attention.

To: Isadora Madsen
From: Stevie Mathews
CC: Nicolas Montgomery
Subject: Re: status?

Liam and Morgan are hypocrites. I'm totally fed up with the way I'm being treated. So I organize a little bit. What parent doesn't want a kid who keeps things tidy?

Hey, Nico. Do you know a guy named Elias? He's finishing his junior year. He told me that he'd seen me hanging around with you before. Anyway, he asked me out for coffee before school when I go back. So I asked my parents, and Liam and Morgan went ballistic. It's bullshit. They get to live by one set of rules, but I have to achieve other standards. This isn't f***ing fair.

Well, I showed them. I ran out on dinner, and

they can beg and plead all they want, but I'm not coming back to the table until I get my way, the right way. I bet their parents had shitfits when they started dating because of their ages. Why don't they understand what I'm up against with peer shit, to begin with? They're supposed to support me through thick and thin, not go haywire over such a minute detail.

Stevie doesn't even put down the tablet when her phone starts vibrating. She looks at who's texting and smiles:

Nico: Elias? R U kidding me?
Izzy: who's Elias?
Nico: he's real good-looking.
Izzy: have I seen him b4?
Nico: he dates cheerleaders. they hang on him.
Stevie: it's casual. just coffee.
Nico: Stevie, *deadpan stare* i don't believe U.
Izzy: so am I to understand where U met?
Nico: he was in the psych ward. *utter disbelief*
Stevie: tell me what U know.
Izzy: everything.
Nico: he brings his car into my dad's car wash.
Izzy: good tipper?
Nico: awesome tipper
Stevie: is he alone?
Nico: not usually...today he was
Izzy: U saw him today?
Stevie: did he say anything today?
Nico: he actually talked a lot

Stevie: about what?

Nico: nothing in particular, pretty chummy tho

Stevie: exactly what did he say?

Nico: about the new soap we're using

Izzy: I don't think that's what she meant

Nico: it was little stuff like the fast food joint fries

Stevie: nothing about any girl, anyone?

Nico: I asked, "no girl today?"

Stevie: And?

Nico: he said, "running free these days"

Stevie: Damn. Parents pounding on door.

Nico: talk to you later

Izzy: I love u guys.

"Stevie," Dad pounds. "Open up the door. You need to eat and take these meds. Damn it, now."

"Fine," Stevie opens the door, takes the tray from Mom, walks it to her bed, returns to take the pills, and lets Mom and Dad watch that she took them correctly.

"Now, you need to eat, or that pill will make you nauseous," Mom says.

"Stevie," Dad is stern. "We need to talk about this boy."

"What is there to say? We both have our own perspectives." Stevie stammers. "My food is getting cold, and I won't eat it cold. Can we talk tomorrow? Thanks. Good night," Stevie closes the door and locks it.

Once she finishes her casserole and breadsticks, Stevie takes the dishes into her bathroom sink and rinses them clean. She then returns them to the tray in an orderly fashion and sets it just outside her door. In the process, she hears that someone is around the corner watching TV in the family room. She peeks around to see a mirrored reflection of Mom and Dad. It sounds to Stevie like they're watching a Hallmark movie again. Those are Mom's favorites.

Stevie backs up quietly into her bedroom and locks the door. She returns to her bed in time to feel the phone vibrate.

Elias: Stevie?
Stevie: I'm here.
Elias: How R U?
Stevie: getting sleepy but good. U?
Elias: catching up on homework.
Stevie: U go back tomorrow?
Elias: Yep, and U?
Stevie: Just the testing center in the morning.
Elias: I might see U there.
Stevie: cool.
Elias: I saw Nico today.
Stevie: how was he doing?
Elias: pretty good, I think
Stevie: do U work?
Elias: parents won't let me.
Stevie: because of OCD?
Elias: The warden won't allow me.
Stevie: I have one of those too
Elias: don't cross him or no car
Stevie: really?
Elias: why the surprise?
Stevie: would've thought a jr has more freedom
Elias: haha
Stevie: I'm kind of fighting with mine

Elias: OCD things?
Stevie: not really
Elias: then give in this time, reap rewards next
Stevie: U got this down to a science?
Elias: not a master manipulator
Elias: if that's what U mean
Elias: U there? Getting sleepy again?
Stevie: maybe a little
Elias: save a dream for me. Nite.

9 Unanswerable Questions

"Stevie, what would you like to accomplish this year here in school. And you can't say finish it," Ms. Willoughby, the school counselor, asks.

"That's all I can think of since I've had a lot on my plate recently."

"But there has to be something more that you want to achieve?"

"Good grades, I don't know. I really have to get to the testing center so I can complete all the tests I have to before I need to leave," Stevie says.

"Okay. But I'm going to talk to you again soon. And I want you to have an answer. Okay?"

"Okay," Stevie replies, leaving her office, grabbing a hall pass from the receptionist, and bumping into the school nurse, Ms. Daniels.

"Stevie, I'll need the doctor's note to give you meds once you return. Can you remind your mom about that?"

"Yes, I will."

Stevie rushes down the corridors and crosses some hallways to get to the library's testing center, where Elias is nowhere to be found. She opens the door and shows her school ID for the tests she needs to take. Each of the four tests has a fifty-minute time limit. She reads the clock on the wall: 8:44 am. Where's Elias?

Students come and go while she's there, but no Elias. Finally, on her last test, he rushes the door. The proctor tells him to calm down and hands him the test that matches his ID badge. Elias takes a seat two away from Stevie at the back of the class in the upper levels of the stadium seating. Elias goes about arranging pens in different orders at the front of his table. The proctor keeps an eye on them: the only two test-takers in the room. Stevie glances sideways to see how far through his test papers he is, so she'll finish at about the same time as him.

"Times up, Ms. Mathews," the proctor yells.

"Okay," Stevie stands and gathers her test and pen, looking sideways the entire time. Elias avoids her glance due to the proctor's stares.

"Now, Ms. Mathews."

Stevie moves slowly, partly due to medications, and to stay beside Elias for the most part. Once out in the library, she takes a seat near the testing center door, but checkout staff whispers and eyes her curiously as Stevie doesn't move once the bell rings for class change. When it appears like one of them is about to approach her, Stevie leaves.

"Stevie," Elias says just as Stevie is about to make her way across the courtyard to the offices and out the front door. "I'm sorry. My test took longer than I thought. Plus, they wouldn't let me out of classes for the longest time. I'm glad that I didn't miss you. Can I pick you up before school tomorrow for coffee, my treat?"

"Actually, I've got the rest of this week off to get used to the sedative, so it doesn't knock me out," Stevie replies. "What about this weekend? We can just meet up at the coffee shop."

"Great, whatever works for you," Elias responds and glances behind her to where the principal walks towards them. "Hello, sir. I was just saying hello to a friend. We were just in the testing center, and both have our hall passes. We'll be on our way now. Sorry." Elias shows the hall pass and nods his head to Stevie, who smiles at both him and the principal before she waves her hall pass and rushes down and out the main doors.

"Stevie, how'd your tests go?" Mom asks, waiting out front in the visitor parking lot.

"Good, how long have you been here?" Stevie questions.

"I pulled in five minutes ago. Why were you waiting?"

"No, it's good timing then," Stevie says, tapping on the center console. Stevie picks up her water bottle and then sets it back down.

"What's wrong, honey?"

"I feel like I'll choke if I drink the water," Stevie says.

"That's insane, sweetie. Take a drink," Mom insists.

"Why don't we stop and get something to eat, and you can get one of those smoothies you like," Mom offers.

"I'll choke on anything. I can see myself choking," Stevie counters. "Mom, something's wrong. I just want to go home."

"Okay, sweetie. We're almost there."

"I'll lie down, and after my next sedative, maybe I can swallow something."

"That's almost two hours away. You need to have water before then," Mom worries.

"Can I take my sedative early? Maybe then I can drink and eat something?"

"Okay, maybe this one time." Mom pulls the pill bottle out of her purse.

Stevie takes the pill and nibbles it into little pieces, which she then crushes between her fingers into the dust, which she holds in the palm of her hand. Stevie then licks the dust and swallows roughly, almost gagging. Mom hands her the bottle of water, but Stevie can't take it yet. As they near home, Stevie reaches and takes a sip.

"Okay, Mom, by the time we get to the drive-thru, I think I might be able to eat a burger with a smoothie."

"Sure, honey. I'm on the way."

By the time they reach the two side-by-side drive-thrus, Stevie is drinking large swigs of water.

"Cheeseburger, fries, and large water, and a strawberry, raspberry, banana, and orange juice fruit smoothie next door, please? I'm starving. I think it's this medicine, but I'm hungry."

"Well, you haven't eaten since last evening. Remember, you were running late and couldn't have breakfast," Mom reminds.

"Thanks, Mom," Stevie chomps on the fries while waiting at the second drive-thru for her smoothie.

"Oh, honey, I hope this doesn't ruin your appetite for dinner. Maybe I shouldn't have given you that pill at this time."

"Mom, chill. Don't worry. You wanted me to eat and drink. I'm doing that. No worries."

After the drive-thru, Stevie sips on her smoothie for the next half hour, almost in a buzz off her meds. Mom helps Stevie down to her bedroom and tucks her in.

"I need my phone and my tablet," Stevie stammers.

"Okay. Here you go, honey. The phone is on the nightstand, and the tablet is beside you on the bed. Good. close your eyes."

When Stevie finally wakes, the house is quiet. She lies there on her back and listens for footsteps. Stevie rolls over and looks at the digital clock on the nightstand, which reads: 7:02 pm. She picks up her water bottle and gags. Then she remembers how the afternoon went.

I can't swallow because I'll choke. It was only after taking the medicine that I was able to swallow again. What the hell is happening to me? How do I get rid of these obsessive thoughts of choking on food or drink? Why do these thoughts all of a sudden pop into my head? How do I get rid of them? Maybe if I distract myself and refuse to think about the thoughts. Maybe that will work. What are Nico and Izzy doing?

Stevie sits up and grabs her phone to read the emails. First from her teachers and then the important ones.

To: Stevie Mathews
From: Nicolas Montgomery
CC: Isadora Madsen
Subject: I saw you.

Tell me everything that happened. I was on my way to my locker with my hall pass when I saw the principal checking you and Elias out. What was going on? Did he catch you guys? Did you kiss? What happened? What did you guys talk about? I saw Elias later and told him that I'd seen him talking to you earlier, and all he had to say was that Mr. Kelly had interrupted you both. So, what were you doing? Elias thinks that you're really nice, classy. Does that mean that you didn't kiss? Tell me the scoop. Did you kiss? Elias isn't the kind to kiss and tell, so I'm dying to know what happened. Later.

Stevie blushes at the thought of a kiss. She deletes a bunch of spam messages until she gets to Izzy's.

To: Stevie Mathews
From: Isadora Madsen
CC: Nicolas Montgomery
Subject: Re: I saw you.

OMG. Tell me, too. Did you kiss? I finally found out who this Elias guy was. I had Nico point him out to me at lunch. Handsome. Nice body. Beautiful eyes. We walked by him, and he waved to Nico. Your mom says the meds are still kicking your butt. She claims you were asleep again when we rang your bell. Shit. Girl. Take your sleepers at bedtime. Where do you hope this goes with Elias? Fill me in. Catch us up. Call. Text. Email. Do something. I'm adrift without you.

Stevie goes into the bathroom and afterward tries to comb out her hair. When it doesn't sit right, she yanks on it. Suddenly, she hears footsteps up above. They are making their way down the stairs, and then a knock on her door.

"Stevie," Mom knocks, then opens it up to find Stevie standing in front of her. "Oh, good, you're awake. Do you want some dinner? I can warm it up for you."

"I don't think that I can again without taking my meds."

"I don't want to give them to you early again. That's setting up a bad pattern, honey," Mom says.

"Well, then I'll have to eat and drink after I take them."

"Honey, you need more water than that," Mom informs.

"I can't, Mom. I don't know what's wrong with me," Stevie cries.

"Maybe the therapist will know tomorrow?" Mom suggests.

"Shelby is just trying to lock me up again. She's waiting for me to say the wrong thing."

"No, honey. Let's give her a try. Why don't we take a water bottle with us and show her what the problem is? Maybe there's a solution?"

"Whatever," Stevie sulks. "I'm going to do some homework until it's time for the meds, then I'll eat some leftovers, okay, Mom?"

"You bet, baby," Mom says as she closes the door behind her, and Stevie listens to the footsteps before she returns to her emails.

To: Isadora Madsen
From: Stevie Mathews
CC: Nicolas Montgomery
Subject: Re: I see you.

Nothing happened. We had just run into each

other when Mr. Kelly saw us, and we showed him our hall passes and parted ways. So nothing exciting. No first kiss. No out-of-this-world moment to report.

Yeah, I was knocked out again. What time did you come by today? I just woke up like fifteen minutes ago. So, Morgan wasn't lying to you guys.

What does classy mean? Goody two-shoes? Does he call the cheerleaders classy? What the hell? I can be bold and out there. In fact, I'm going to text him right now. Later.

Stevie flips through the messages from Dad, Piper, cousins, and Grandma on her phone to find the one from Elias.

Stevie: what's up?
Elias: there U R. Been thinking about U.
Stevie: really?
Stevie: what about me?
Elias: how beautiful U R
Stevie: no, I'm not
Elias: yes U R and I'm not just saying that
Stevie: U R around so many beautiful girls
Elias: checking me out? *blushes*
Stevie: I'm just saying
Stevie: why bother talking to me?
Elias: bcuz UR not just pretty, UR nice
Stevie: I think U must know other nice girls
Elias: you'd be surprised how catty they R
Stevie: what R U doing for Memorial Day?

Elias: family reunion pavilion lakeside
Elias: would you like to come?
Stevie: Umm
Elias: pls. it won't be worth it w/o U
Stevie: I'll ask Nico and Izzy
Stevie: is it okay if they join me?
Elias: the more the merrier
Elias: Nico's cool
Stevie: so is Izzy
Elias: please make sure, beg them for me
Stevie: Nico thinks UR cool too
Elias: talking about me *blushes again*
Stevie: get over ur self
Elias: I'm just joking. But I want U there, pls
Stevie: I'll try.
Elias: do U know of the OCD group on Thurs
Stevie: where?
Elias: the counseling center conference rm
Stevie: where's that?
Elias: off the main lobby, the double doors.
Stevie: oh, they've always been closed
Elias: different groups each night
Elias: OCD on Thursdays at 8pm
Elias: Lucy from the ward goes
Stevie: really? Lucy?
Elias: she's nice
Elias: there's a few OCD groups around
Elias: I like that one the most
Stevie: why?
Elias: facilitator keeps it on topic, no cliques
Stevie: where do U sign up
Elias: just show up
Elias: or if Ur a patient the therapist puts u on list
Stevie: so I could go this Thurs night at 8pm

Elias: U bet, C U there? I got to go now
Steve: I'll try. Bye
Elias: Bye

May 24rd, 8:19 pm

Basement Bedroom
Dear Journal,

I'm making progress with Elias, I think. But what's this? It's a picture of Elias and me on my socials. The principal is in the background. Somebody snapped us with our hall passes. It's from one of the junior varsity cheerleaders. I bet it's Elias's former girlfriend. Holy crap! There's more from other cheerleaders. They've written all over my page: 'slut', 'tramp,' 'brazen little hussy.' Why would they do this to me?

10 The Gentle Art of Making Enemies

"It's Sensorimotor OCD," Shelby says.

"So, it's OCD as well?" Morgan asks.

"Stevie, why are you so withdrawn today? You usually speak your mind."

"It's nothing," Stevie responds.

"So, this inability to swallow for fear of choking doesn't bother you?"

"It does. I just have other things on my mind that are more important."

"Tell us, sweetie," Mom nudges.

"It's nothing," Stevie reassures.

"Ms. Mathews, can I speak to Stevie alone today?" Shelby asks.

"I'd rather not," Morgan replies.

"It's okay, Mom," Stevie responds. "I'll be fine. Really."

"Okay, I guess I'll go out and wait in the waiting room," Morgan mopes.

"She's gone now. Will you tell me what's on your mind today?" Shelby prods.

"Can I join the Thursday night OCD group here in the conference room?" Stevie spurts.

"How do you know about that group?" Shelby asks.

"A friend from the hospital told me about it," Stevie reveals.

"A female friend?" Shelby questions.

"No, not necessarily."

"I facilitate that group on Thursday nights," Shelby informs. "Who told you about it?"

"Elias."

"Nice boy."

"Is he?"

"You must know him if he told you about the group?"

"Just brief conversations, one of which ruined my life," Stevie sulks.

"How is that?"

"Someone took a picture of Elias talking to me in school after the testing center and posted it on my socials with disgusting names," Stevie frets.

"Somebody is jealous of you," Shelby alerts.

"I didn't do anything. He was just saying hello. That's all."

"It's probably one of Elias's ex-girlfriends. It would be best to talk to the counselor at school, and they'll deal with it in the administration. That's bullying." Shelby elaborates. "So, I'm getting the vibe that you haven't told your parents about Elias."

"Actually, I have, but that didn't go well," Stevie says.

"What happened?" Shelby notes on her tablet.

"They said that I couldn't see anybody from the hospital. Not those people."

"Ah, I see," Shelby pauses. "So, you'd like to see Elias in the group because you can't see him out of school or in school either, for that matter?"

"Partly, I'm interested in the group because another hospital friend goes there too. Her name is Lucy," Stevie informs.

"Ah, yes, nice young lady," Shelby assures.

"But I'm curious as to what you talk about with OCD-related stuff."

"I can put you on the list for tonight. You just show up a few minutes before, since we start directly at eight and run until nine. We stay on topic, so you won't be able to talk to either of them until afterward if you stay for fellowship, where we meet next door in smaller groups at the coffee shop for an hour, just until they're about to close."

"He asked me to go to his family reunion on Memorial Day. It's at the park's lakeside picnic pavilion. I asked him if I could bring my friends, Nico and Izzy, with me. Elias said, Sure. I can't tell my parents about it, though," Stevie says.

"Is that a good idea, lying to them? What happens when they find out?" Shelby is curious.

"Shelby, I can't tell them. They're hypocrites," Stevie sniffles.

"How do you figure?"

"There's a five-year age gap between them, and they are balking at a two-year age difference between Elias and me," Stevie stammers.

"It's more pronounced at a younger age, Stevie," Shelby says. "Your parents are only looking out for your best interests."

"No, they're treating me like a child. I'm not a child. Look at what I'm dealing with: this OCD and being in a psych ward. This isn't childish stuff. I'm old enough," Stevie spiels.

"So, what is it that you hope that happens at this reunion?"

"We talk." Stevie is flustered. "I don't know. I'll be with my best friends, for Chrissake's."

"Okay, well, I suggest that you talk to your parents. You knew I was going to say that. But I do hope that you come to the OCD group tonight. You should warn your parents that Elias will be in attendance."

"I can't. I just can't," Stevie stands her ground.

"So what am I supposed to do about the choking images that prevent me from swallowing?"

"Okay, so there's ERP, which is short for Exposure Response Prevention, and it belongs to the category of treatment called cognitive-behavioral therapy. It's a form of psychotherapy meant to help those with obsessive thoughts, such as the images of you choking, to hold off from responding with compulsions or rituals. It does this by gradually exposing you to spurs that prompt your gagging response and avoidance," Shelby elaborates.

"So, what exactly do I do?" Stevie asks.

"Keep trying to drink from the water bottle. Get a little further each time until you can take a sip, knowing that the images will be bold, but you can take them on, and if you keep it up, eventually you'll be able to drink despite battling the thoughts."

"I don't know if I can do that," Stevie admits.

"We'll talk about it in the group tonight. I promise." Shelby says.

"Well, I'd better get going. My time is up, and my mom is waiting. Thank you, Shelby."

"So, what did you two talk about in there?" Mom asks.

"Nothing, really, oh, there's an OCD group here tonight that I told her I'd check out. It's in a conference room off the main lobby. And afterward, there's fellowship at the coffee shop where everyone breaks into smaller groups and talks about what the session did or meant for them. It's at eight."

"Oh, okay. I'm just thinking about the timing of your medication to keep you alert for the group.

Plus, you'll want to have dinner beforehand," Mom thinks it out. "Maybe take your meds at two, then have lunch and nap."

"Sounds great."

"I'll make you a chicken salad. Until then, maybe get caught up on your reading and assignments," Mom suggests.

After three hours of studying, Stevie takes her pill crushed up again and manages a sip of water after eight tries. Once she succeeds in swallowing the pill, it's only a brief amount of time before she can take her salad, then she is down for a nap.

"Stevie, it's been four hours. You've been sleeping this whole time. You need to wake up and have dinner if you want to attend that OCD group at the counseling center," Mom nudges Stevie awake.

"Dad, it's good to see you," Stevie says, performing her usual setting the table rituals after washing and scrubbing her hands eight times.

"So, tell me about this OCD group. Who'll be there?"

"Shelby, my therapist runs it and a bunch of people with OCD."

"So, you learned about this through your therapist?"

"Yes," Stevie lies.

"So, honey, what was the deal about Mom not being able to sit in your therapy session today?" Dad prods.

"I don't know. Shelby wanted to talk to me alone," Stevie says.

"What did you have to say that you couldn't tell Mom?"

"I just answered Shelby's questions, and she told me how I could get over my choking fears and not do the rituals."

"I see," Dad puts his hands out for a hug.

"Can you wash up correctly, Dad?"

"I'll try."

"Hey, Piper, how's it going?" Stevie asks.

"Good. When are you going to be used to your meds so I can talk to you again?"

"Well, you can talk to her at the table right now, Piper," Dad says.

"Dad," Piper balks.

"Soon, I promise. Each time I take the sedative, it works a little less. So, I shouldn't conk out all the time. Then we can have girl talk."

"I don't like all these secrets everybody has," Dad pouts.

"But the meds should still have a little oomph to get you through this meal, correct?" Mom questions Stevie.

"If I hurry, I think I can get some soup down," Stevie responds. "Then I got to get ready to go to group."

"What's to get ready for? You just go and sit and talk?"

"Well, I don't want to look like I just rolled out of bed, which I just did," Stevie replies. "Mom, can we leave at 7:30? I don't want to be late. Shelby says that it starts promptly at 8:00."

"Sweetie, I've got work to do. So, Dad will be dropping you off and picking you up, okay, honey?" Mom asks.

"Sure." Stevie starts tapping the table.

"We can leave at 7:30. Not a problem," Dad

responds.

Stevie's tapping continues on the middle console while Dad drives her over to the counseling center.

"Honey, are you worried about something?" Dad inquires.

"Dad, I tap, shake, and fiddle at everything. Nothing special," Stevie says.

"Okay, honey, so I'll pick you up outside the coffee shop at ten."

"Yes, Dad. I got to go," Stevie rushes into the lobby of the counseling center, where she runs into both Elias and Lucy.

"Hey, guys," Stevie beams. "Lucy, it's good to see you again," Stevie says.

Once inside, Stevie takes a seat between Lucy and Elias. She's surprised to see Marvin from the hospital is in the group, too.

Oh, look, Marvin's waving at me. I'll wave back. And there's that other guy from the hospital group. I know he's twenty-eight, but I can't remember his name. Now he's waving. Better wave back. I've got to figure out his name, or something bad is going to happen. I need to recollect his name on my own. Now my damn knee is shaking. I look as bad off as the guy to the left of us tapping his knee in four sets. Henry. The guy next to Marvin's name is Henry. Crisis averted. This time anyway. Oh, there's Shelby. Shit. She looked at me, then Elias. He's going to know that I've been talking about him to her in therapy.

"Okay, everyone. It's the top of the hour, so we

should get started. Tonight, I know we have two new people in the group. You can either volunteer an introduction, wait a little bit, or chat with others in fellowship, coffee at the shop next door immediately after our group here or forego it altogether."

Henry shakes his head, so Stevie does, too.

"Okay, then tonight, I wanted to focus on sensorimotor OCD, like choking fears, and how we overcome them with ERP. Would anyone like to share their experience with the group?"

"Hello, everyone, I'm Ed, and I have sensorimotor OCD in that I have obsessions with blinking and breathing. If any one of a multitude of things happens or is said, I have to blink to erase it. For example, if someone says a curse word, then I have to blink three times, and then the obsession goes   away."

"No, Ed, that's giving in to the obsession by performing the ritual," Shelby says. "Instead of giving in to the compulsion, how would we use Exposure Response Prevention to handle the obsession?"

Marvin replies, "By allowing it to be present? Is that what you're talking about?"

"Exactly. Embracing the awareness of the bodily process," Shelby says. "Thank you, Ed and Marvin. Does anybody else have a sensorimotor obsession and compulsion to share with the group?"

"I think one of mine isn't. It kind of depends on the doctor that I talk to sometimes, it seems," Elias adds. "Mine involves awareness of my heartbeat, especially when still, like in a quiet classroom or when I'm lying down."

"In the case of heartbeat, some doctors feel it's more panic disorder related, but we can include it in our discussion tonight," Shelby says. "What kinds of things have you learned to help you with your compulsion?"

"Well, instead of counting my heartbeats or tapping to get rid of them. I mean, I know I can't get rid of them, but tapping five times helps me focus on the tapping as opposed to the counting. But I know the answer you're looking for, Shelby, is doing the body scan."

"Exactly. Thank you, Elias," Shelby nods. "Does anyone else care to contribute? And possibly share with the group what the body scan is."

"My sensorimotor OCD involves my macular degeneration. I mean, I don't have macular degeneration, but I see floaters in my eyes, and then I have to count them or wave them back down three times," Lucy shares. "And with the body scan, we start by shifting our awareness to body parts, processes, or like sensations. We begin with our head or our toes and work our way through the body, welcoming the sensations."

"So, with the body scan, we start with a relaxed posture. Sometimes, it's preferable to be lying down, but it can be done anywhere. Then we'd start at the top of our head this time and focus on the awareness of our hair, then the scalp, forehead, eyes, and if your obsession involves your eyes, really focus on welcoming the awareness of, say, floaters, as in Lucy's share. Spend time with the floaters, mentally greet them, and tell them that it's okay that they're there. Or with Ed's share, let's focus on our blinking process by welcoming it. Then go on to the nose, focus on the nostrils; next is the mouth, be aware of the structure, then the processes like saliva production and swallowing. Invite the processes. Just be with them. Then we go to our neck, and shoulders, then chest, spending time focusing on each. Next, it's the heart, and with Elias' share the focus on the heartbeat. If you can't feel it, then maybe take your pulse on your wrist for this part. Truly welcome it. Interact with it by calming the breath. If you're breathing heavily, then invite that and be at one with it. Whether it's fast or slow, it's doing its job. Accept it. Then move on down the body. You can do this alone, lying down or sitting up in your doctor's office lobby, being silent and still."

"And what is the end goal with this body scan?" Henry asks.

"Excellent question, Henry. Welcome to the group," Shelby replies. The end goal is to decrease anxiety through welcoming the awareness without trying to avoid it by doing some ritual."

"Is this the same thing as mindfulness?" Henry questions.

"Does anybody know the difference?" Shelby inquires.

"Mindfulness just focuses on the sensory preoccupation that you're here for and doesn't go throughout the whole body like in the scan," Marvin responds.

"In my case, it's like focusing on breathing through the sensation of air going through my nostrils or the rise and fall of my chest, and the goal isn't to judge but to accept with curiosity and focus of the moment," Ed says.

"Same end goal?" Henry wonders.

"Yes, a fading or tolerance of sensory focus of the preoccupation," Shelby responds. "Well, we're almost at the end of this meeting. It goes so fast when we do the body scan or partial scan. It was an excellent group tonight. I hope all of you come back next time, and as usual, there will be fellowship in the coffee shop next door. Attendance there is not necessary. It's just a time to introduce yourself one-on-one or in small groups. Next week, we'll go into introductions here. It was good seeing all of you. I'll be here for a few minutes for any questions before I join any of you who want to meet next door."

Once inside the coffee shop, the members of the group line up for their orders. Elias offers to buy Stevie her mocha Frappuccino, so she takes a seat in a booth nearest the window.

"Oh, crap, Dad will be able to see in," Stevie whispers to herself as she's about to move to another seat. One of the group members who didn't speak up approaches her.

"Hi, there, I'm Sally. I'm in the OCD group and sit across from you," a woman past middle age greets Stevie.

"Oh, hi. My name is Stevie. I'm waiting on Elias and Lucy. If you want, you can take a seat," Stevie offers.

"Sure, thanks. I don't speak up all that often in a large group. I'm a little shy that way," Sally confesses.

"So long have you had OCD?" Stevie asks.

"I have what's called "pure O," which is obsessions without the need for compulsions that prevent bad things from happening to you or your loved ones."

"Really, that's interesting," Stevie says. "How long have you had it?"

"For about fifteen years, I think, give or take, but I've only been treated for the last five. Shelby's actually my therapist. I've been in this group as long as she's been leading it," Sally elaborates.

"So you're not new to the body scan?" Stevie asks.

"Oh, no, been doing that for a long time. It's very relaxing. I worry one of these times I'll fall asleep," Sally admits. "Besides relaxing me, it doesn't do all that much for me like some of the others."

"Hey, Sally," Lucy says as she sits next to her.

"Hi there, we were just talking about the body scan. Hi, Elias. It's nice to see you came back." Sally adds, "I hope you don't mind that I joined you guys. I was chatting with Stevie here."

"Not at all," Elias lies.

"No, it's great," Lucy says, stirring her coffee. "Hey, Shelby, pull up a chair and join us."

"Okay, I'll do that right after I order."

"I'm glad Shelby talked about somatic OCD tonight. It was helpful," Lucy says.

"I thought it was called sensorimotor OCD," Stevie is curious.

"They both mean the same thing in referring to the body and its processes," Sally pipes in, causing Lucy to roll her eyes. "I should run to the bathroom. Excuse me, Lucy. Don't talk about anything interesting while I'm gone."

"Not a problem," Lucy replies and slides out of the booth. Once Sally is out of earshot, Lucy says.

"That woman just rubs me the wrong way. Every time I meet someone new in the group, she welcomes herself to the conversation and then hogs it. What she should be doing is speaking up in the group. She waits until we get in here and lets loose. God damn. Give someone else a chance to speak."

"Yeah, I noticed that last week," Elias adds. "I didn't want to say anything, so I'm glad you did. I didn't want to make enemies."

"Oh, allow me to do it," Lucy fumes until Shelby pulls up a chair at the end of the booth.

The next hour flies by quickly, and Shelby leaves to say goodbye to the other small groups first. Then Lucy gets up and leaves. Sally doesn't take the hint when Elias changes the conversation to school. She keeps coming back with group gossip. It's only when Stevie has to leave that Sally gathers her things as well.

"Yeah, I should be going, too," Sally says. "It was nice talking with you guys. It's always nice to have new blood in the group to get to know. Thanks for letting me join you guys."

Stevie stays at the end of the booth near Elias for a second. "Thanks for the Frappuccino, Elias."

"My pleasure. I only wish I had more time to chat with you and not Sally."

"No kidding. I see what Lucy meant," Stevie says. Then she sees her dad pull up out front. "I'd better go, though. My dad's here. I'll text you, okay?"

"Sounds great. Goodnight, Stevie."

11 Of Thorns and Roses

"Stevie, that's not the boy from the hospital that we told you specifically that you couldn't meet at a coffee shop, is it?" Dad fumes.

"It turns out he's in my therapy group. It's not like I was meeting him alone. There were three other people at that table before you drove up, one of whom was the group leader, Shelby," Stevie responds.

"We gave you specific instructions to stay away from him, and you were sitting right beside him," Dad yells.

"I'm sorry, but I didn't have a choice," Stevie lies blatantly.

"So, you couldn't have sat somewhere else?" Dad asks.

"Everyone in there has the same problem. So what difference does it make who I sat next to? The other groups had older men in them. Would you rather I sat and talked to them because I met them at the hospital, too?" Stevie explains.

"We'll see what your mother has to say about this manipulative act," Dad responds.

The rest of the ride home is in silence. After Dad pulls into the garage, Stevie exits, slamming the door. Dad follows suit shortly afterward, and they meet Mom in the kitchen. She's relaxing, sipping hot cocoa, and paging through a magazine.

"Dad is pissed off at me because the boy from the hospital was in my group tonight, and I sat in the same small group with him at the coffee shop, along with Shelby, Lucy, and Sally," Stevie steams.

"Did you know he was going to be there?"

Mom wonders.

"No, I didn't know anyone from the hospital would be there," Stevie lies. "But I'm glad they were…all of them…so it didn't feel so uncomfortable. As it was, I didn't speak up because I was nervous, and that's frowned upon. But knowing they're not total strangers may make it easier for me to speak next week."

"I guess there isn't a problem with that," Mom says, surprised.

"What are you drinking? Of course, there's a problem with this because we told her specifically not to see that boy," Dad stammers.

"If she didn't know and couldn't have prevented it, I don't see how we can hold it against her," Mom sides with Stevie.

Dad throws his hands up in the air, "I don't know what the hell is happening here. And let me go on record that I don't totally believe this was a chance meeting." Dad rushes up the stairs.

"You should go to bed and get some rest," Mom says. "But first, let me give you your meds." Mom slides Stevie a bottle of water. Stevie kisses Mom goodnight, goes to the front door, and strokes the coins on the string with the back of her hand eight times, then disappears down the stairs to her bedroom, where she checks her email.

To: Stevie Mathews
From: Nicolas Montgomery
CC: Isadora Madsen
Subject: OCD group

How did it go tonight? Was it helpful? Say,

you'll be in class on Tuesday for certain, right? Because we have the baby pig dissection lab. That's like a quarter of our grade with all the worksheets and all. I'm just saying, I hope nothing happened tonight to interfere with you coming back to school.

Stevie scans through some marketing emails to find Izzy's response.

To: Stevie Mathews
From: Isadora Madsen
CC: Nicolas Montgomery
Subject: Re: OCD group

How can you be so insensitive, Nico? She's dealing with some heavy shit. Give her some space. Oh, crap, the study hall monitor is walking around to make sure that we're working on school work and not playing games or emailing friends. Gotta go.

Stevie leans back against her headboard and sighs. She checks her phone for possible text messages from Elias, then responds to Nico and Izzy.

To: Isadora Madsen
From: Stevie Mathews
CC: Nicolas Montgomery
Subject: Re: OCD group

It was an enjoyable group and fellowship afterward in the coffee shop. Elias sat next to me. It was intense, even though three other people sat in and around us. We really didn't get a chance to talk until the end. He didn't say much except that he'd text me. So I've got that to look forward to, I guess. You guys are still taking me to his family's reunion at the lakeside park on Monday, Memorial Day, correct? This is going to be great.

Stevie tosses her phone and laptop to the side and wipes tears from her eyes. She lies back and thinks:

Shit. I hate lying to Dad, but he didn't give me any option. They were so irrational in the first place. I mean really, what's the difference between me talking to anybody with OCD and me talking to Elias? They're just ignorant. They're denouncing Elias for his OCD. That's totally unfair and not cool. But once I go to Elias' family reunion, that is really stepping outside the bounds. There will be no going back from there. Granted, they shouldn't be able to find out about it, but I know deep inside that it's not right. I wish they wouldn't corner me this way. It gives me no other choice but to deceive them. I feel guilty, especially since Mom was on my side tonight. Crap.

May 25th, 11:01 pm
Basement Bedroom
Dear Journal,

It's official. I've got a crush on the cutest guy in school. Plus, I think that he likes me, too. Too bad my parents think he's a nutcase. Wait a minute, if they think poorly of him. Then what does that say about their feelings for me? And now I'm outright deceiving them. Once I go to this reunion picnic, there ain't no going back from that as I will have blatantly lied to them both. But what other options?

I'm going around in circles and getting lost in my thoughts. The medications seem to be working on the sedative side, but not on obsessions and compulsions. I'm just getting better at hiding them. The downside to the group is that I can watch what other people are doing and then emulate their actions, so I'm not as noticeable. Is that what my life is going to be like from now on: hiding my compulsions and placating my obsessions?

I overheard Sally telling Lucy about blood pressure medication used to treat anxiety, but it's not for women of childbearing age, at least those not actively trying to get pregnant. Does that mean that due to my diagnosis, I can't have children? That would be crappy. I mean, I don't want them now, but sometime in like ten to fifteen years, maybe. Will my OCD go away or be more manageable by then?

After an uneventful weekend, mainly spent trying to stay caught up on school work so I can return on Tuesday, it's finally the day of the reunion picnic for Elias' family. Mom and Dad think that I'm going to the park with Nico and Izzy, who also have nothing else going on besides their families grilling out in the backyard, the same as mine. They're supposed to pick me up at 11:30 am.

"Hey, Nico, thanks for driving," Stevie says as she runs out to the car after stroking the back of her hand against the coins on the entry door ten times.

"My pleasure," Nico replies. "All I would've been doing is chillin' with my family, whom I've seen all weekend. I've missed you and Izzy."

"Didn't you hang out while I was in the hospital?" Stevie asks.

"No, it just didn't feel like us with you missing. I think it put us in a funk. But that all over now, right? You're back to school tomorrow," Nico spurts.

"Yeah, I'm so anxious about going back," Stevie admits.

"To school or the psych ward?" Nico asks for clarification.

"Both, honestly," Stevie responds. "I don't want to deal with all the peer crap in school. It's so much added pressure. My mom contacted the school about the bullying, and those girls got in trouble, but I don't think that I've heard the last of them yet," Stevie says.

Nico squeezes Stevie's shoulder, "Buddy, battling mental illness should be enough on your plate. You shouldn't have to deal with stigma or jealousy with Elias, whatever their problem is."

"Thanks, Nico."

"You bet."

"Now, where's Izzy?" Stevie looks around the front yard of her other best friend's place.

"She said she was ready like fifteen minutes ago," Nico informs. "And she's hyped. So where the hell is she?"

Just then, Izzy bounds out the front door towards Nico's car and climbs in the back seat.

"What took you guys so long?" Izzy spurts.

"We've been waiting for you out here for ten minutes," Nico stammers.

"You took so long. I had to pee." Izzy retorts. "So is this trip to the park still on the down-low?"

"Yup," Stevie bursts. "If they're going to look down on my friends with OCD, then they're looking down on me as well. That means they're pretty much forcing my hand to lie to them."

"It comes down to respect," Nico says. "When my parents disrespect me and my wants, then how can they expect me to fall in line?"

"I just hope that you don't get caught," Izzy replies.

"There's no way," Stevie smiles.

Once they pull into the lakeside park's lot, it's full to the brim, so they have to park across the street in an overflow lot. In the process, they cross paths with Stevie's dad's coworker John and his wife, Jessica, who is also one of Stevie's mom's closest friends. They wave Stevie over.

"Oh, shit," Stevie whispers.

"Stevie, we're surprised to see you here. How do you know the McIntyre family?"

"Ah, I know Elias from school. Nico here

does, too. He invited us to stop by for a little bit," Stevie stutters.

Elias's mom comes over to greet John and Jessica. At about the same time, Elias greets Stevie, Nico, and Izzy.

"Stevie, Nico, Izzy, this is my mom, Adelaide. Mom, this is Stevie from the hospital and her friends. I told you about her," Elias says.

"Hello, Mrs. McIntyre. It's nice to meet you," Stevie sputters.

"Likewise, and please call me Adelaide. I've heard such nice things about you," Adelaide turns to John and Jessica and apologizes, "I'm sorry. This is my son's friend from the hospital. I didn't mean to ignore you guys. Well, thank you all for coming. I hope that you have a wonderful time, each and every one of you." Adelaide takes Jessica's hand in hers and pulls them towards the picnic pavilion.

John and Jessica take a quick glance back at Elias before they turn to follow Adelaide into the huge group of people lined up for burgers, brats, and hot dogs. There are numerous hamper-sized buckets filled with ice and sodas, but John and Jessica stand in line with the beer tap, each looking back at Stevie.

They know full well I just lied to their faces. John and Jessica are definitely going to spill the beans to Mom and Dad. Oh, well, I guess that I'd better make the best out of this day as possible. Elias seems awfully fidgety today. In fact, it looks like his hands are shaking. This is looking all too familiar to me.

"Nico, I think Elias may be having an OCD episode. He just looks really anxious. Don't you think?" Stevie says. "Hey, Elias. Want to take a walk with us before we eat?"

"Stevie, no, I can't. Everything's messed up. Entirely in disarray, don't you see?"

"Elias, please come with me for a walk?"

"Stevie, the roses aren't in a perfect line. See that one. It's askew," Elias focuses.

"The little rose bushes are beautiful." Izzy chimes in to help her friend.

"No, that one is definitely out of line," Elias says, climbing into the garden, kneeling down, and digging with his hands, which are being cut up.

"Elias, everyone is looking over here. I think that you should get out of the garden," Stevie says quietly.

"Stevie, I think we should go," Izzy nudges. "Nico, do something."

"Elias, hey buddy, come on. Let's get out of the garden. You're getting gashed. Man, people are looking at you," Nico prods.

"Oh, crap. His mom is coming over here, and she looks pissed."

"Adelaide, I think Elias—"

"Get the hell out of here—all three of you. Elias was just fine until you showed up," Adelaide yells. "And don't come near my son again." She tries to pull on Elias, but her resists, getting bloodier and dirtier by the minute. Not to mention the sweat rolling down his face in the ninety-degree full sunlight.

Stevie hesitates, which angers Adelaide, who turns towards her husband and demands that he remove Stevie, Nico, and Izzy.

"Come on, guys, I think it's enough for today.

Why don't you be running along now, okay." Elias's father pushes them along while Elias continues to make a mess of himself and his mother, both of whom are rolling in the blood and the sweat and the tears. Onlookers rush over to help remove Elias, pull him over to one of the ice buckets, and wet him down, cleaning some blood off in the process.

As Stevie, Nico, and Izzy back away slowly, other onlookers wave them away, which has Stevie bawling and wiping her eyes. She searches the crowd for John and Jessica and makes eye contact. They turn away. Stevie rushes behind Nico and Izzy to his car parked across the street. Not watching where she's going almost gets her run over, but she pounds on the hood of the car that nearly kills her. They pull out of the lot facing the picnic pavilion, where dozens of faces stare in their direction. Nico squeals out of the lot and down a different path. Izzy, all the while holding Stevie in her arms in the backseat.

When Nico drives up to Stevie's house, her parents rush out and pull her from the back seat. Stevie's tears stream down her legs as she falls to the stamped concrete driveway, thereby muddying up the blood and the dirt from the garden she was just pulled out of when she tried rescuing the cutest guy in school.

"John just called us," Dad stammers. "Stevie, what were you thinking? We warned you that a boy like you would be too much for a relationship. Why doesn't anyone listen to me?"

"I'm sorry, Mom, Dad," Stevie sputters. "I thought we were both okay."

12 Running from the Past

"I'm sorry that happened to you, Stevie." Shelby offers. "Is there anything I can do for you?"

"No, I guess that my parents were right all along," Stevie replies.

"I don't believe they were right. I feel the same about Mrs. McIntyre. She shouldn't have made Elias's episode about you. I think she must have overreacted and gotten a little embarrassed, and she just took it out on the person closest in proximity," Shelby says.

"I think that if I had a kid, I wouldn't want her to be friends with someone like me either," Stevie sobs. "I really liked Elias. And I was trying to help him. The movements looked and felt so familiar. I sensed he was going to have that episode. Mrs. McIntyre got it all wrong. I wanted to help him. I didn't care about all those other people."

"Well, why don't we wait and see the fallout from that episode. At this point, I think the emotional wound is still too deep for everyone involved."

"So, then what else are we going to discuss?" Stevie asks.

"I know there was something I wanted to touch on. Where's it at in my notes?" Shelby swipes her tablet while Stevie wipes her eyes. "Oh, here it is. You have a strong aversion to certain shades of blue. Why is that?"

"I don't know," Stevie shrugs.

"Surely, that shade must remind you of something." Shelby prods.

"Dishes, I guess. My grandma's dishes. I think she called either the color or the pattern Wedgwood. It's close in value to country blue or maybe a pale azure, maybe? It's the color of a kiddie pool."

"Do you have fond memories of your grandma's house?"

"Not particularly, I guess. No."

"Why is that?" Shelby delves.

"I don't know because I love my grandma dearly. She is so kind. She wouldn't hurt a fly," Stevie says.

"And your grandfather?"

"He died a few years ago. But he was kind as well," Stevie recalls.

"Do they live in the country?"

"Edge of a small town up north, so yeah, I guess," Stevie says.

"Do you have chores when you go there?" Shelby wonders.

"No, why do you ask?" Stevie is curious.

"I guess it's nothing. I still wonder what the aversion was to the blue rug. I just wanted to know what drove you to such anxiety," Shelby says. "It's rather unusual to dislike a set of dishes so much that you carry it with you through the ages."

"I guess that I didn't like sleeping there when they babysat us," Stevie replies. "Not Piper, she wasn't born yet, but my cousins and I when we were younger, and my grandpa was still alive."

"Were you like all crammed in a room?" Shelby prods.

"No, some of the older kids camped outside. We younger ones slept in the guest bedroom,"

Stevie recalls.

"Did you guys play until all hours of the night? That's how I remember sleepovers with cousins," Shelby says.

"No, we—"

"What were you going to say?" Shelby wonders.

"My uncle made us fall asleep early, but—"

"What is it, Stevie?"

"My grandparents would go to bingo at the casino. So, my uncle would come over and watch us until they got back," Stevie shares. "We'd act up so he'd give us younger ones that green cough syrup that would knock us out and—"

"And what?" Shelby asks. "That doesn't sound like an appropriate reason. Were you sick?"

"No, we—"

"What are you thinking about, Stevie?"

"I…I don't want to talk about it," Stevie stutters.

"I think you should get it out. Stevie?"

"I think that I don't like my grandma's dishes because of my uncle," Stevie pauses. "He'd babysit us when grandma and grandpa went to the casino, and his wife went along as well. My aunt was never there with us. The older kids were always outside camping in that big old tent. They'd take out soda and water and chips so they wouldn't have to come inside and bother my uncle because he said he was reading, but—"

"Stevie? What was your uncle doing?"

"Nothing."

"Stevie, you're holding something back from me," Shelby says.

"I don't want to talk about it," Stevie stands her ground.

"Okay, okay, we can talk more about it next time. Would you like to talk more about Elias? The reunion picnic? Your parents' response?" Shelby attempts to change the subject.

Stevie begins crying.

"Stevie, what's going on?" Shelby wonders. "We can talk about whatever you want to discuss. Your choice."

Tears stream down Stevie's face.

"Why did they leave me with him? And my cousin McKenna, she—"

"What happened to your cousin McKenna?" Shelby asks.

"That medicine made us so sleepy. We didn't even—"

Stevie pulls her knees up to her chest and cries into her hands. Shelby offers more tissues. She just sits with Stevie and lets her bawl.

"I've got to get to class now. I'll be late," Stevie says.

"We'll talk on Thursday. You're next appt. is at 7:00 am; then I'll see you that night in the group, okay, Stevie?" Shelby reminds.

Stevie exits and walks down the corridor to the waiting room, almost in zombie-like form.

I'm numb to the fuckin' world. What just happened in there? Where did all that drama come from? Why did she push on the stupid color of the dishes? Why didn't McKenna tell anyone? Why did they make me stay overnight there? I remember telling them that I didn't want to sleep at Grandma's. Couldn't they tell that we were loopy from that green cough syrup? What the hell is happening? I can't deal with this crap right now.

Stevie walks past Mom in the waiting room and out to the elevator while Mom rushes to catch up.

"Stevie, how'd that go? You seem like you're in a daze," Mom asks.

"Why did you leave us at Grandma's back then? I told you that I didn't like sleepovers there?" Stevie stammers.

"What? Because your dad and I wanted some alone time together to go on some little day trips that you wouldn't have cared to go on with us? Why do you ask?" Mom replies. "What do you mean by 'we', because Piper never stayed there with you?"

"McKenna and me. And Josh and Joey? We were left alone in the guest bedroom while the older cousins slept out in the tent," Stevie recalls.

"Why are you bringing this up now?" Mom wonders.

"Never mind. I'm going to be late for school," Stevie stutters.

"Forget about Grandma and Grandpa's. Did you talk to Shelby about Elias?" Mom asks.

"Not much. I think that Shelby might want to talk to you about what happened," Stevie informs.

"Why would she want to talk to me?"

"Because you and Elias's mom reacted the same way. You looked down upon each other's kid like the other one messed up or might mess up each of your little angels, and that's not the case. We're in the same boat, Mom. Elias is me; I am Elias. We have obsessive-compulsive disorder. We're trying to get better, but our parents blame each other's kid for something that lives in their own home. Mental illness is a part of your family, Mom. It's a part of their family. I disagree that it's my fault or his. We're trying to get better and grow up through peer crap at the same time. It's difficult enough without our parents going batshit crazy over our misdoings," Stevie elaborates.

"Shelby said that?" Mom pauses.

"Not in so many words, but she would like to talk to you," Stevie relays. "I need to get to school before I'm late. Nico will have a fit if I miss our dissection lab this morning."

Once in the Biology lab, things start off fine. There are whispers and giggles from across the room where Heidi Godsey, Shawna Sway, and Jade Zwirdle sit, but Nico's bolstering Stevie's attitude helps big time. The little pigs lay on the trays atop the lab stations awaiting work. The instructor is reviewing details and adding any final instructions on how the lab will proceed.

"Any last-minute questions before we begin?" Mr. Chalberg asks.

One of the football players, Les, over by Godsey, Sway, and Zwirdle raises his hand, "Yes, Mr. Chalberg, I was wondering if Stevie Mathews needs to stand up and sit down; eight times before we begin? We can all wait for her." The class erupts in laughter. "Look at her, eight different colored pens all lined up on her desk. What a weirdo! She's got a weirdo boyfriend, too." The class continues to laugh while Mr. Chalberg tries to yell over the top of it all rather unsuccessfully.

"Yeah, Lester Littleshit Louwagie, you're really

fucking funny. Do you want me to come over there and kick your five-foot-tall fucking ass?" Stevie stammers while each of them raises their middle fingers to each other as the class starts to caw and cower.

"It's Les Lipschitz Louwagie, you psycho bitch. You can come over here and try," Les says.

"You really want me to go psycho on your ass?" Stevie stands up and rushes towards him, and he crouches behind Mr. Chalberg, who intervenes and chases both Stevie and Les down to the principal's office while the rest of the class begins the dissection lab.

After a brief wait for Mr. Chalberg to relay the incident, Stevie goes in first and lashes out at Les's inciting words, "Is it okay for a privileged football player to demean a mentally ill student in front of the class? I'm sure my parents and our family lawyer would like to know your answer, as I was only standing up for my dignity despite a class full of laughter caused by Les. And this is after bullying I received from students at this same school for the same mental health disorder. What's your response? Please be clear, as I will relay it to my parents and our family attorney." Stevie shrugs her right shoulder to her right ear eight times in a row.

"Please wait out by the receptionist's desk while I speak to Mr. Louwagie," the principal says.

About an hour later, Liam and Morgan Mathews arrive to defend their daughter, who had already texted the details of the incident to them. As they're leaving with Stevie, the Louwagie parents brush elbows with the Mathews and apologize for any misunderstanding. Stevie gets suspended for the rest of the day, while Les gets a three-day suspension. His parents, meanwhile, will introduce further punishment at the Mathews' request.

"Here are your things, Ms. Mathews," Mr. Chalberg says as he hands Stevie the belongings that she left in the classroom, which she immediately wipes down with wet wipes.

"Stevie, it doesn't matter what someone ridicules you with about your mental illness; resorting to violence is not allowed, do you understand?" Mom asks.

"I wasn't really going to hurt him. I just charged at him to scare the tiny jerk," Stevie smirks. "Mom, he called me a psycho bitch. I would show the class and him just what this psycho bitch can do to him and their laughing asses. You honestly didn't expect me to roll over and cower, did you? I do have a smidgeon of self-respect left."

Lester Lipschitz Louwagie can just kiss my ass. I'm not about to let that little pipsqueak make fun of me. Yes, I have to put up with junior cheerleaders and even Godsey, Seay, and Zwirdle's whispers and giggles, but any outright defamatory is going to be met with a swift response. No, I won't be violent. But hell if I'll let them mock me in front of a group. I'm going to have enough self-respect to set things straight.

Dad pulls the extended cab truck into the driveway, and Mom rushes out the door and into the house while Stevie grabs things. Dad gets Stevie's attention and holds out his fist for a fist bump. Stevie smiles.

"Good verbal responses on your part. But no

physical interaction, okay, sweetie?"

"Sure, Dad," Stevie says.

"Now get in there and do some studying. I have to get back to work for a few more hours at least," Dad says.

Stevie: I got suspended for the rest of today.
Nico: really? shit. I started dissection.
Stevie: how did it go without me?
Nico: for me, fine. class was quiet.
Nico: even Godsey, Sway and Zwirdle
Stevie: did I make a scene?
Nico: U put him in his place.
Stevie: now everyone knows I'm crazy.
Nico: everyone already knew that.
Nico: now they know U stand your ground.
Izzy: wtf, I just heard
Nico: Stevie lurched at his ass
Izzy: wish I could've been there
Izzy: everyone's talking about it
Stevie: I just had enough
Izzy: jr cheerleaders even talking about it
Nico: R U going to go to summer school
Stevie: shrink wrote me a note, so NO
Izzy: can we come over after school?
Stevie: probably not, Mom is upset about it
Nico: I heard they stood up for U
Stevie: to the principal, but scolded me
Izzy: for what?
Stevie: getting violent
Nico: U didn't touch him, he was hiding

Stevie: he was, wasn't he 😊
Izzy: LOL
Nico: LMFAO

Stevie searches the kitchen drawers for a straw. Her swallowing obsession is in full force.

"Sweetie, if you're looking for a straw, they're in the cupboard to the right of the fridge," Mom says.

"I just wanted to say again how sorry I am for lurching after Les. Please don't be mad, Mom," Stevie apologizes.

"I'm not mad. The little shit deserved it. I just don't want you fighting," Mom grimaces. "I don't want you running from anything, but I don't want you to have battles in the first place. I'm just sad. I don't know what I'm saying. I'm just glad you're safe and that his little ass is frightened of you, so maybe no more incidents like this one."

13 Looking Forward to the Future

"Thank you for joining us today," Shelby tells Liam and Morgan Mathews. "I just wanted to chat briefly about the things that have transpired with Elias and his mother."

"I don't care what you say. You're not going to get me to change my mind about that boy," Dad challenges.

"Do you see that you're treating Elias the same way in which his mother treated your daughter at the picnic reunion?" Shelby points.

"My daughter was wrong to attend that gathering," Dad admits.

"Your daughter was mistreated in the form of being yelled at and told to leave for something that wasn't her doing. Is that really okay with you? Once you see that, then you'll see that the way you're treating Elias is just the same," Shelby says.

"So what, because you think so, we're supposed to let our daughter date a lunatic?" Dad sputters.

"I'm a lunatic too, Dad," Stevie adds.

"You can get better. He's gone off the deep end, acting like he did at that family reunion. John and Jessica told us that he was down digging in the garden, all bloody and sweaty," Dad says.

"Dad, I just got suspended from school for violent behavior."

"What?" Shelby's stunned. "Wait. What's this?"

"It's nothing. Someone was calling me names in front of the class, and I charged at him, but he cowered behind the teacher, so all was well. I got suspended the day, and he got suspended three days," Stevie informs. "Back to Elias…."

"Okay," Shelby is hesitant. "Back to Elias, I'm not suggesting you let your daughter date Elias. I'm just saying that you need to look at the situation with open eyes. The things Elias is going through are the same things that your daughter is dealing with. Different obsessions and compulsions, but the same disorder."

"We just think where you put your focus is what you get in return," Dad fumes. "We want our daughter to have a better chance in life."

"We aren't talking wedding, Dad. We just want to be friends," Stevie says.

"Friends going out for coffee, meals, or entertainment is a date," Dad spurts.

"I do those things with Nico."

"That's different," Dad replies.

"How?"

"Izzy is in attendance," Dad counters.

"Not all the time," Stevie stammers.

"What do you want from us, Stevie?" Dad sighs and falters.

"I want to be able to have mentally challenged friends, whether it's illness or disability. I want to be able to go to a coffee shop or to dinner or out to a movie with friends who are different," Stevie spiels.

"What do you think, Morgan? You haven't said a word," Dad asks Mom.

"I guess that I'm open to trying it out," Mom replies.

"Okay, then. We'll try it out. Can I go now? I need to get back to work?" Dad asks.

Shelby nods, and Dad leaves.

"Mrs. Mathews, could you wait out in the lobby so I can have the rest of the time with Stevie?" Shelby asks.

"So, how do you feel about this blowup at school?" Shelby asks Stevie after Mom exits.

"I returned with a little more respect," Stevie replies.

"Respect or fear?"

"I don't know, but definitely a little more self-respect for sure," Stevie admits.

"So they learned they couldn't just make fun of you, and you'll take it?"

"I guess not. So, thank you for helping open my parents' eyes to the similarities between Elias and me. Now I can join you in the group again tonight and fellowship afterward," Stevie smiles ear-to-ear. "Even if Elias doesn't make it because he might still be in the hospital, it doesn't mean that I won't be there. I like hearing about things that other people have learned to cope with this disorder."

"Yeah? You liked the body scan?" Shelby wonders.

"Definitely."

"Maybe tonight you'll introduce yourself?"

"I'll try my best. I think our time's up. I should go. Same time next Tuesday?" Stevie asks.

"Yes, and I'll see you tonight." Shelby waves goodbye as Stevie sees herself out.

The lab test in Biology goes off without a hitch. Nobody even looks her way when Stevie uses baby wipes to wipe down the desk before sitting, then standing eight times, then organizing her eight different colored pens in the order of the rainbow. She looks out the window and thinks.

English class is even respectful, and they're usually boisterous in here before the teacher comes in. On a more personal note: I don't know why I even carry the water bottle anymore. I'm getting less abled to drinking it without a straw. The medication isn't working as well as it did, if that even was the case, considering the placebo effect. Did I just think I was doing better at first because I was taking a pill?

Stevie raises her right shoulder to her right ear eight times, then begins blinking her eyes in the quietness of the room. Suddenly, she just closes her eyes and holds them tightly shut until she hears the teacher. When she reopens them, the teacher is trying hard not to stare in her direction.

Lunch is uneventful. It's obvious her classmates are trying to ignore her. Giving her space is a welcome reprieve from the gawking. Whispers and giggles are still heard, but only lead to further paranoia if given attention.

Spanish with Izzy and Nutrition with Nico round out the day. Elias is nowhere to be seen. Not that she gets the best chances since they're in different grades and classes. By the time Mom pulls up at the curb to pick her up, Stevie is in a pretty good mood, looking forward to the remainder of the day.

Dinner went well tonight. With the exception of the 'we're trusting you to respect us with your actions' crap. Mom and Dad just want to instill fear in me, so I'll align with their expectations. All in all, it's pretty good that they'll let me be friends with Elias, whom I hope shows up tonight. Even if he was on a seventy-two-hour hold, he should be out by now. But if he'd told his mom he knew me from OCD group, she may not allow him to attend. I realize what he had was just an episode and that it wasn't the real him. Oh, I hope, I hope, I hope he's there tonight.

"Stevie, remember we love you," Dad says just before Stevie steps out of his truck.

"That was ominous," Stevie whispers to herself.

Stevie enters the building and heads straight to the conference room, where she finds familiar faces sitting in a circle awaiting Shelby.

"Stevie, come and sit by me," Sally offers.

"Oh, hi Sally, have you seen Lucy or Elias yet this evening?" Stevie asks.

"No, and they're both usually here before me. Go figure," Sally says.

"Hello. Everyone. I'm on time, but just barely. How is everyone this week?" Shelby tells the group. "Well, it looks like we have a couple of new faces, and we're missing a couple of people, too."

"Are we doing introductions tonight?" Marvin asks Shelby.

"Yes, we are." Shelby sighs while looking at the clock on the wall. Just then, the door opens, and Lucy enters, looking a little disheveled. She sits next to Stevie. Henry follows her in and takes a seat over by Marvin.

"Okay, then, let's get started," Shelby says as Elias barrels through the door and pulls down an extra chair, and sits beside Henry.

He doesn't make eye contact with Stevie.

"My name is Shelby, and I facilitate this group. Some of you are my clients and already know me. To all of you, welcome to the Thursday night OCD group. Maybe we can go around the room, and each say our name, and since we are all here because of OCD, why don't we tell the group something about us that isn't OCD-related? Perhaps a talking point for when we meet afterward at the coffee shop next door for fellowship, which is not mandatory. I'll start. I like to crochet and sew quilts in my spare time."

"I'm Marvin, and I read about ten books a month for enjoyment."

"I'm Henry. I love numbers, so I went into accounting and own my CPA service and work out of my home."

"Hello. I'm Elias, and I'm a football player at my school, where I'll be a senior next year."

"Hi, I'm Zoey, and I go to the same school as Elias, but I'm graduating next week. I'm going to college for interior design.

"Hello, everyone, I'm Deidre, and I have four cats and a dog. My two kids are in college, so the animals are my fur babies now."

"Hey there, I'm Trevor, and if you miss a week around here, a half dozen people show up and a few disappear. It's nice to have a full group, though. I like going to my family's cabin up north and swimming, fishing, or snowmobiling in the wintertime."

"Hello. I'm sorry I was late. I'm Lucy, and I just graduated from college. I like to paint in my spare time."

"Ah, hi, I'm Stevie. And I'll be a sophomore next year, and I really enjoy writing short stories and journaling."

"Everyone, hello. I'm Sally. I, too, have four cats, no dog. I live alone. No kids. I enjoy collaging and papercrafts."

"I'm Lane, and I have my own residential construction business. Hello, everyone."

"Well, hello, everyone. I'm Ed Finley, and I'm a tile setter, and I enjoy throwing pots and firing up the kiln for fun."

"Okay, everyone, it's nice to have you all here. Is there anyone who wants to share something that happened to them this past week? Or ask a question about something they heard about OCD that they'd like the group to discuss?"

"Yes, I was wondering what the difference is between OCD and panic attacks or anxiety disorder because I sure feel anxious and feel panic-stricken at times," Trevor asks.

"Does anyone have an answer for Trevor?" Shelby asks. "Yes, Marvin."

"Well, as far as I've read or heard, it depends on the behavioral component, in that we with OCD typically engage in compulsions or rituals to cope with our anxiety and panic. That's different from an anxiety disorder, which is worrying about life stressors, not arrangements, or orderliness, or other obsessions," Marvin elaborates.

"And panic attacks feel like heart attacks, sudden, terrifying fear that's felt physically, and they don't have obsessions or compulsions either," Ed says.

Zoey raises her hand, "Can I ask what the difference is between my body movements and tics or twitches?"

"Twitches are isolated actions, like a jerky movement. Tics are uncontrolled movements or a series of actions that the sufferer can't manage on their own. I think it comes down to behavioral component again in that we can use our rituals to control our movements, gestures, or actions," Deidre says.

"And what is a productive way to deal with the repetitive movements of OCD?" Shelby asks the group.

"Progressive muscle relaxation, like the body scan," Lucy replies.

"Yes," Shelby responds.

"Exercise and yoga?" Zoey asks.

"Absolutely, yoga and meditation are extremely beneficial," Shelby says.

"How about one nostril breathing or lower diaphragmatic breathing in four and out six counts?" Marvin wonders.

"Excellent. Would you like to show the class how we do that for those who haven't seen it done before now?" Shelby asks Marvin.

"Well, one nostril breathing is simply closing off one side of your nose when you breathe in, then switching to the other nostril to breathe out," Marvin reveals.

"And what is its purpose?" Shelby asks.

"To focus on the breath instead of our obsessions. Mindfulness and living in the moment where we're not wrapped up in our obsessions and compulsions," Marvin says.

"Does anybody else know what the lower diaphragmatic breathing in four and out six counts means?" Shelby looks around the group.

"It's when you inhale to the count of four, all the way down to your diaphragm, and then you're slower on the exhale to a count of six, for a deep, relaxing breath, which is also living in the moment and focusing on the breath," Lucy says.

"Why don't we try these for a little bit while I send around a sheet for your name, phone number, and email address so I can contact you should something come up, and we won't be meeting a certain week. That way, you won't drive here for nothing in the event group is canceled," Shelby suggests.

"Is it mandatory?" Lane asks.

"Of course not, give what information you feel comfortable with everyone," Shelby clarifies.

After some one nostril breathing and lower diaphragmatic breathing exercises, the group readies to go next door to the coffee shop. The few laggies hang behind to chat with Shelby as usual. Stevie pays close attention to Elias, who is shaking Marvin and Henry's hands and looking like he is cutting out for the evening.

"What's his problem?" Lucy whispers to Shelby.

"I don't know. Maybe he's mad at me?" Stevie says.

"Girls, don't whisper. It's rude," Sally responds.

"We're whispering because it doesn't concern anybody else, Sally," Lucy stammers. "I'll go talk to him." Lucy squeezes Stevie's arm.

"Come on, Stevie, let's go to the coffee shop," Sally nudges.

"I'll be right there. I'd like to wait for Lucy," Stevie hangs back.

"Suit yourself. I'll save you a spot." Sally informs.

"Hey, Elias, what's up?" Lucy asks as she reaches him curbside in front of the counseling center.

"Not much; how about you, Lucy?"

"Aren't you coming to the coffee shop?"

"Not tonight. No," Elias replies.

"Is there something wrong? I think Stevie feels like you're mad at her for something," Lucy says.

"No, I'm not, really. I'm partly ashamed and the other part disappointed."

"Disappointed in Stevie?"

"No, our parents. They spoke to each other by phone and had a shouting match. Stevie's parents think I'm too crazy for her, and my mom thinks Stevie's to blame for a recent episode I had in front of Stevie, which is why I'm embarrassed," Elias shares.

"I don't think anything has changed for Stevie. If anything, she's a little worried that she's losing a friend," Lucy suggests. "Maybe talk it out with her before you take off and leave her wondering what she did wrong."

"Okay, here she comes," Elias points and waves Stevie over.

"See you next week, Elias," Lucy responds.

"Thanks, Lucy." Elias turns to Stevie, "Hey, there?"

"Hi. What's going on?"

"I'm sorry about the picnic episode. First of all, I'm ashamed of my behavior. I didn't take my meds for a couple of days because they were really dragging me down, and I wanted to be alert and remember the fun time we were going to have at the picnic. I should've known better," Elias says, waving goodbye to Shelby and Marvin as they cross paths on their way over to the coffee shop. "Do you know that our parents talked on the phone?"

"No, I didn't know that," Stevie fumes.

"Yeah, your parents don't like me very much and want me to stay as far away from you as I can. They threatened not to allow you to attend the group if I was present. I thought about staying home tonight, but I really wanted to see you, even if I couldn't speak to you."

Stevie's fingers start flexing. Elias reaches out and holds her hand. Stevie looks at him with a few tears streaming down her face.

"Don't cry, please," Elias says.

"I'm angry with my parents. They should've told me they spoke with yours. I had a session with Shelby and me, and she made it clear to them that you and I are no different with our disorder. My parents gave in and said that you and I could be friends," Stevie sputters.

They continue to hold hands.

"I heard about your threatening to kick Les's butt in school," Elias laughs. "Good for you."

Elias squeezes Stevie's hand. They smile, then look away to see the whole coffee shop staring at them, and then turn away.

14 The Danger of Things Left Unsaid

Stevie fiddles around with her phone, tosses it to her bed, then paces the floor in her bedroom. When she returns to her phone, she lets out a big sigh, then zeros in on a text conversation.

Stevie: Hey, McKenna. How R U doing?
McKenna: Hi there, cuz. What up?
Stevie: Just hoping my texts aren't hijacked.
McKenna: No parental units here.
Stevie: Mine R targeting this guy I met.
McKenna: That's shitty.
Stevie: I know, right.
McKenna: Is he cute?
Stevie: Incredibly…and older.
McKenna: Like a man?
Stevie: he'll be a senior next year.
McKenna: parents would go ballistic.
Stevie: So I was wondering about you?
McKenna: What about?
Stevie: Just a little flashback sort of thing?
McKenna: How am I involved?
Stevie: Remember sleepovers at Gram's
McKenna: I do. I miss Pops.
Stevie: Do you remember Uncle Bob?
McKenna: Smarmy old fucker.
Stevie: How do you figure?
McKenna: Just the sense.
Stevie: Remember that green cough syrup?
McKenna: Oh, yeah. Had forgotten about it.
Stevie: Adults think he is funny.
McKenna: Josh and Joey hate his guts.
Stevie: What about him do they hate?

McKenna: He has different personalities.
Stevie: I guess so.
McKenna: Why do U care now?
Stevie: He came up in therapy the other day.
McKenna: How so?
Stevie: the green cough syrup
McKenna: wanted us asleep, so he could drink
Stevie: was that it?
McKenna: he kept older kids locked outside
Stevie: yeah, I remember that.
McKenna: Gram would've kicked his butt
McKenna: if she knew he drank while babysitting
Stevie: I do remember him dancing with us
McKenna: He was drunk and held us
Stevie: Yeah, I remember that too
McKenna: gotta go, cuz
Stevie: another time, bye

Stevie tosses the phone to the bed and pulls her hair in frustration. She tries finger-combing it to perfection, but the strands are unruly. Stevie yanks on roots until Mom calls down for breakfast.

"Hey, sweetie, have you been sleeping in?" Mom asks.

"No, I was texting McKenna," Stevie relays.

"That was nice. What did you talk about?" Mom wonders.

"Just the sleepovers at Gram's," Stevie shares.

"Why the fixation on those sleepovers, sweetie?" Mom prods.

"Fixation on what sleepovers?" Dad asks, coming down the stairs for breakfast.

"Nothing important, honey," Mom snaps.

"Just about Uncle Bob," Stevie tells, merely poking at her food.

"I don't like Uncle Bob," Piper adds.

"Piper, that's my brother. Be respectful," Mom snaps back.

"But he's creepy. And he smells like sweat and beer," Piper continues. "His kisses are disgusting."

"Exactly," Stevie spurts. She pushes her plate forward.

"Enough," Mom orders. "Eat your breakfast."

"What do you girls have planned today?" Dad changes the subject as he glances at a fuming Mom finishing her plate early and cleaning up the table.

"I'm going to buy another radon kit for the basement because I don't think the electric one is working," Stevie replies while putting the napkin over her eggs. "Then I'm going to go with Elias, Nico, and Izzy to the nearby lake. They've got a diving platform there, plus they rent pedal boats and canoes at the other end of the beach."

"First things first. We don't have a radon problem. The detector works. Secondly, who's driving? You know how we feel about a bunch of kids cruising in a car with the radio blaring. It's very distracting and can cause an accident. Finally, is there a lifeguard on duty?" Dad asks.

"Yes, to radon. Elias is driving. No to blaring music and distraction, and yes to the lifeguard."

"Okay, did you take your meds, Stevie?" Dad asks.

"Mom?"

"I'm working on it, Stevie," Mom is distracted.

"And you, Piper? What are your plans for

today?" Dad wonders.

"Going across the street to play in Violet's pool," Piper replies.

"Hey, did McKenna mention how Josh and Joey are doing?" Dad slips.

"Stop the gossiping, please," Mom demands with a harsh tone.

"What's wrong with Josh and Joey?" Stevie asks.

"Not now, honey. Your mom would like us to stop the chitter-chatter about the relatives," Dad obeys Mom's request.

Piper is next to leave the table, then Stevie cleans up in an orderly fashion using the spray disinfectant last.

"Stevie, I'm still eating. Enough with the spray," Dad barks.

"I think that I've got non-Hodgkin lymphoma. I read about it. Its precise name is MALT-lymphoma. It states that mainly older adults develop it after a lifetime of exposure to chemicals in various products, but teens can also contract it. I think from spray disinfectants and that carpet freshener you put down before you vacuum. It gets up into the air, and we breathe it in," Stevie spiels.

"I'm not trying to kill you with chemical particles if that's what you're insinuating, Stevie," Mom snaps.

"I'm going to go down and clean my room," Stevie goes to the front door to brush the feng shui coins with the back of her fingers eight times. Then she bounds downstairs, catching a bit of a conversation between Mom and Dad, who think Stevie's out of earshot.

"Liam, don't encourage the girls to gang up on my brother, Bob. He's had a difficult life. We've all tried to lessen his burden, so encouraging the girls to poke fun or insinuate things is not helpful. I don't know where Stevie is going with the sleepover comments. Do you know she told her therapist about them? Just imagine what repressed memories that witch is trying to stir up? Remember how she got Stevie on a psychiatric hold by mingling words. We've got to stay on the same page with this, Liam, please?"

"Wait, a minute, Morgan. What the hell are we talking about with Bob and the sleepovers? What did Stevie say?" Dad stammers.

"Nothing. Stevie said nothing. I just want to keep it that way and not have the girls startle Gram. She's finally come back to normal since my dad died," Morgan says, wiping down the countertops.

"Morgan, if anything, no matter how slight, may have happened at those sleepovers, I want to know, regardless of how this affects your mother, or Bob, for that matter," Dad puts his foot down on the matter. He turns and walks upstairs.

Stevie stands still against the wall at the bottom of the stairwell, still listening up into the kitchen, where Mom is crying and sniffling. Stevie steps quietly into her bedroom and leans against the back of the door. She stands there looking around at the orderly bedroom and starts yanking on her hair.

"Stevie, you forgot your meds. They're on the counter. I'm going upstairs to change," Mom bellows.

Stevie opens the door slowly and climbs the stairs, void of any emotion. She gets into the kitchen, picks up the pills, and reaches into the fridge for a bottle of water. After she swallows them, she picks up the bottle of sedatives whose label reads: Take one three times daily. Stevie shakes the bottle, then pauses and opens it up. She pours a handful in her palm, waits again, then returns the medicine to its bottle and tightens the cap.

"What the hell am I doing?" Stevie whispers. Just then, her phone vibrates in her back pocket. It's a text conversation.

> Nico: So what R we supposed to do?
> Nico: make ourselves scarce?
> Izzy: Yeah, do U want alone time with Elias?
> Stevie: No, don't go making it obvious.
> Nico: I thought we're just UR cover story
> Stevie: I want you guys there, too.
> Izzy: Okay, it'll be fun
> Nico: How R your parents handling this?
> Stevie: Who's to say what they're thinking?
> Izzy: Whoa? Argument?
> Stevie: No, my mom is just batshit crazy
> Nico: is this about Elias?
> Stevie: No, therapy crap, just forget about it.
> Izzy: Okay
> Stevie: That's what she wants me to do.
> Nico: Stevie, R U ok?
> Stevie: I'm fine. I'm excited. Let's do this.

Steve returns to her bedroom and changes in and out of about ten outfits before she settles on a yellow polka dot string bikini with a light baby blue tee with white lettering over the top and some white shorts and sandals. She looks at her watch and rushes to hang or fold her clothes in an orderly fashion. Stevie's rearranging the shoes in the cubbies of her walk-in closet when the doorbell rings. She goes to her bedroom door and flips the light eight times, then exits. She rounds the corner from the stairwell to the foyer at the same time. Dad opens the door and greets Elias.

"Hello, Elias," Dad is somber.

"Hello, Mr. Mathews," Elias is respectful.

"Okay, Dad, we're going to take off now," Stevie says.

"Wait, you're mother would like to meet this young man." Dad pauses, then yells up the stairwell. "Honey, Elias is here to pick up Stevie."

Just then, Piper bounds down the stairs and into the foyer.

"Hello. I'm Piper."

"I'm Elias. Nice to meet you, Piper."

Piper giggles and smiles at Stevie, who playfully musses Piper's hair.

"I'm coming. Just a second," Mom says from the stairs. "Hello, Elias. It's nice to meet you finally."

"My pleasure, Mrs. Mathews," Elias says, fidgeting and blinking.

"Well, we should be going," Stevie gestures Elias out the door, but stops to stroke the feng shui coins with the back of her fingers eight times.

"I'm sorry for them fussing over you," Stevie says to Elias, who holds his front passenger side car door open for her.

"You look beautiful, Stevie," Elias says, stretching his hands five times. "I did just take my medicine, so hopefully, we're looking at a better day to be had by us all."

"I took mine, as well. To be honest, I almost took more," Stevie shares.

"Why is that?" Elias is concerned.

"My mom and I got into a disagreement," Stevie wipes a tear from her eye.

"May I ask about what? Was it me again?" Elias wonders.

"No. Some past stuff came up in therapy with Shelby. I started to tell my mom about it, but she wouldn't have any of it," Stevie discloses.

"Well, that doesn't sound helpful. What does she expect you to do? Keep it in, where it builds and builds until you have an episode," Elias says.

"Typically, she says, let it out or let it fester, but not this time. I was pretty much told to keep it bottled up inside me," Stevie replies.

"Can you talk about it to your dad?"

"I tried talking about it with a cousin who I believe went through the same thing, but she got flighty at the last minute. And then, my dad shared that my other two male cousins were having a difficult time with something. Dad brought it up at the same time I was about to open up. I wonder if it's related. What do you think that I should do?" Stevie asks.

"Personally, I'd have to investigate all sides or options. I'd definitely ask Shelby for her opinion and maybe run with that. I know it would only make my condition worse if someone, especially a parental role model, told me to bottle something up inside. That's batshit crazy," Elias says.

"I know. Right. That's exactly what I said," Stevie fumes.

"Is this the right address?" Elias asks.

"Yeah, Izzy should be out in a minute. Thank you for listening to my crap," Stevie says.

"Anytime. Seriously. Anytime. Day or night. Do you understand?" Elias asks.

Stevie nods her head and then waves to Izzy, who barrels out the door and into the back seat of Elias's car.

"And then Nico is just two blocks away," Stevie informs. "Turn right, here."

After picking up Nico, they drive out to the park with its extensive walking and biking trail system to the East and the big lake to the west, where all the water activities take place.

"How about we go for a bike ride first?" Stevie suggests.

Everyone is in favor, and they head on over to the campground where they rent bikes out at the office. Then they cross back over the highway to the head of the trail system, and they're off on their way. A few miles into it, they slow down for a day camp full of kids running along the paved path. Further down, they slow for a trio of riders on horseback. Nico's chain breaks at the end of the six-mile path, which isn't all bad since he only has to push his bike across the highway and back to the campground's office.

Next up, they trek across the park's playground and picnic pavilion areas to get to the beach rental office, where they check out a canoe and a pedal boat.

"You guys should take kayaks out, which are faster," Izzy suggests.

"No, I think we want to chill and talk a bit,"

Elias says. "Is that okay with you, Stevie?"

"Well, do you want to take the canoe, and we'll get kayaks?" Nico jumps into the conversation.

"Okay, we can take the canoe. You guys rent the kayaks," Stevie puts in her thoughts.

After about an hour of paddling, the waters get rougher on the big lake, which is busy with jet skiers rousing the wake. They return their rentals and shed some clothes on the beach to rush and swim out to the busy diving platform on the campground side of the beach. The other end was overflowing with pickup trucks sliding their boats into the water for a day of fishing. Izzy and Nico raced a bit back and forth to the platform, which gave Elias a chance to sneak in a first kiss for Stevie. Then they sat on the back edge of the platform, snuggled up to each other, completely lost to the world.

15 The Ghosts of My Past

"You shouldn't have opened up a hornet's nest," Mom spews. "Now we have to go up there and fix this."

"Morgan, what the hell are we even talking about here?" Dad worries.

"Nothing's wrong, Mom. McKenna is okay. I'll talk to her. Everything will be fine," Stevie indulges her mother.

"I'm going to gather some healthy snacks for the road trip up to the cabin," Mom disengages.

"Stevie, come here," Dad whispers when Mom is out of earshot. "If there is ever a problem, you know you can talk to me. Even if you're mom isn't on board with discussing it for whatever reasons she's telling herself, I just want you to know that you can always come to me, okay?"

"Thanks, Dad, I'll keep that in mind, but for today, I'm fine. Really." Stevie replies.

"Stevie, why is Mom like flippin' out?" Piper asks.

"She's just afraid of the family getting flustered over things in the past," Stevie whispers.

"What things?" Piper wonders.

"Nothing for you to worry about, sweetie. Just have fun with the cousins when we get there. It'll all be okay," Stevie promises.

The road trip takes three and a half hours to get to serious lake country, where populations increase tenfold when the dusty cabins are unzipped and the furniture dusted off so families can gather together for summertime fun. The only problem for the Mathews-Tarvin-Atkinson-Javery clan is that this isn't a welcome weekend.

"McKenna, what the hell?" Stevie asks. Their other cousin, Kennedy, a few years older than them, leaves the room rather slowly, almost hovering.

"I messed up. I got wasted, drove home from a party, parked on the front lawn, and was crawling around looking for a necklace that fell off when they found me," McKenna replies.

"Then what does this have to do with me?" Stevie responds.

"Our text conversation got me thinking about things back then with the green cough syrup, and I just wanted to blot it all out for a while and not remember it," McKenna sobs.

"I'm sorry, but it was clearly my mind going into a mental breakdown again. I should never have brought you into the mix. Your memories were your own, and I shouldn't have thrown my repressed thoughts on you. But you've got to get over this now. Your mom is going off on my mom, and shit is raining down on me," Stevie elaborates.

"Don't you think we should tell them?" McKenna stews.

"I don't know. Give me some time to talk to my therapist about it all. So, I'm getting the impression that you remember all of it," Stevie questions.

"Maybe that's why Josh and Joey are all fucked up, too?"

"So, what's the deal with them?" Stevie queries.

"They've been drinking pretty non-stop since they turned eighteen a few months back. They are yelling, slapping, kicking, and wrestling pretty roughly. Mom's asked them what's wrong, and they look at each other with contempt, obviously holding something back," McKenna shares.

"So, what makes you think it has anything to do with our recollections?"

"Josh has been in therapy for a year now," McKenna says.

"Goddamn therapists," Stevie fumes. "Bringing all these ghosts back."

"So, they know we're talking right now. What do we tell them when we go back out there?" McKenna wonders.

"Nothing."

"Nothing," McKenna questions.

"Well, we can't say it's nothing, especially if we plan on coming out and telling them what happened back then sometime in the future. And I really can't get into it now before I go over it with my therapist to make certain it is how I remember it," Stevie states.

"If it's as bad as I'm recalling, then you remember it correctly, Stevie."

"Again, so what do we say to them?"

"We throw it back on them. If they ask us to try and explain, we just ask them what they want us to say. We can go round and round forever until they just leave us alone," Stevie declares.

"So, we stick together?"

"You bet. And I'll get back to you after I speak with my therapist," Stevie settles.

The older cousins attempt to pry details out of Stevie and McKenna, but they stand their ground. Meanwhile, Josh and Joey get into a fistfight that perplexes the parents. All in all, a slightly elevated Mathews-Tarvin-Atkinson-Javery family outing.

On the way out, Josh stops Stevie and asks, "So did you convince her to shut the fuck up? Is that really your place to do so?" He says, then turns around, kicks a can out into the street, and disappears around the corner.

Dad appears, "Stevie, if there's anything you need to tell me, then I'm here for you."

"Not at this time, Dad," Stevie pauses, "But thank you. I'll keep it in mind."

"Is McKenna okay?" Dad wonders.

"For now," Stevie says.

The afternoon BBQing goes off without a hitch, then everyone loads up their vehicles for the three-and-a-half-hour ride back to the metro area. Little do they know that the next week will bring changes for everyone and not simply the end of the school year. Piper even senses something's up with Stevie and lays off the annoyances that are part of the sisterly bond. Stevie rushes down to her basement bedroom and fires up her laptop, readying for a journal post, but first, Izzy pops in with a text.

Izzy: R U back from up north, Stevie?
Stevie: Yup, just returned
Nico: What was that all about?
Izzy: family drama?
Stevie: can I ask you guys a question?
Nico: Yup
Izzy: Yeah
Stevie: Would U tear apart UR family
Nico: ?
Stevie: just to save yourself?
Izzy: Clarify, pls

Stevie: past shit, misdoings by someone
Stevie: would U bring them out in the open
Stevie: to keep from going crazy?
Izzy: are U the only one saved?
Stevie: No, others, too
Nico: heavy shit
Stevie: Yes
Izzy: How do the others feel about it?
Stevie: they're prepared to talk
Nico: then U aren't just saving URself
Stevie: I guess not. It feels like it, though.
Izzy: what does UR shrink say?
Stevie: I'll find out on Tuesday.

Stevie sits on her bed, relaxing her head back onto the headboard until she hears footsteps leading down into her room. It's Mom with clean laundry.

Mom's bouncing around like everything is right with the world again. Little does she know that her daughter is stewing about a situation that will bring down the family to the depths of despair. What the hell am I thinking? Do I even have the guts to do it? But Izzy is right. It's not just about me. I have McKenna, Josh, and Joey to think about now, too. Something is definitely up with those boys. I don't remember the details with them. But I do recall the screams of McKenna. Mom is all smiles. She's humming a tune with delight. Talking will tear her apart. But I have no other choice.

June 4th, 9:29 pm
Basement Bedroom

Dear Journal,

So, I went about the next couple of days like nothing happened.

Then talk to Shelby and ask for advice.

Deep down, I know it doesn't matter what she says; it has to come out.

I don't think there's anything anyone can say to stop it.

But what about Gram! This upheaval will devastate her.

Maybe the adults can keep it from her.

Not a chance in hell.

I should tell Dad after I discuss it with Shelby.

But then Mom might resent me for going behind her back.

What do I do about Mom?

Shelby. Have Shelby help me tell Mom.

It's a plan.

Tuesday doesn't come soon enough. Usually, these 7:00 am therapy sessions find me yawning repeatedly. But not today. I'm alert and focused on the task at hand. Mom drives along with all smiles and humorous chitter-chatter, which my mind is all but blocking out. I almost can't even look at her. I'm about to move forward with ruining her life.

"Stevie, do you need me in there? If not, I might sit in the coffee shop and wait for you, sweetie," Mom asks.

"No, I'm good," Stevie counters. She goes inside the counseling center, checks in with the receptionist, then takes a seat and waits until Shelby comes out and calls for her.

Once in Shelby's office, Shelby asks, "So what's up? I'm getting the distinct impression that you're stewing about something."

Stevie goes about telling Shelby the past Sunday goings-on up at the cabin up north, where all of the Mathews-Tarvin-Atkinson-Javery band got together to protect Gram from utter devastation.

"So, what you're saying is that all the parents know what happened but are choosing to turn a blind eye to it all?" Shelby inquires.

"Yes, I think," Stevie replies.

"First things first, let's put aside everything with McKenna, Josh, and Joey and focus on you, just you," Shelby dictates.

"What do you mean, just me?"

"What do you remember? Let's delve into that first," Shelby says. "I want to be clear as to what we're talking about here and not beat around the bush."

"Where do you want me to start?"

"From the beginning, what do you remember?" Shelby notes on her tablet.

"All of our parents, the aunts, and uncles, would get together at Gram's place up north. It was before they collectively purchased the cabin for our get-togethers. We'd have a big BBQ after swimming—Gram lives lakeside. The older kids had a volleyball net up while we, the younger ones, played with dolls or matchbox-sized cars closer to the adults. Uncle Bob, who doesn't have kids of his own, would show up late, already buzzed," Stevie shares.

"Did he focus on you kids?" Shelby inquires.

"No, he pretty much acted like we didn't exist when the other adults were around. He'd eat alongside the adults. His wife would talk gossip with all the others, but he'd just stick to himself most of the time until after dessert, when the whole lot of them would ready themselves for a night at the casino for gambling and bingo, once in a while, the odd concert. Nobody paid much attention to the whines of us kids begging that they didn't leave us there. It was all merriment on their part," Stevie explains.

"Go on," Shelby instructs.

"Then Uncle Bob would have the older ones gather snacks and sodas to take out to the tents the guys were assembling out back near the water's edge, farthest from the house. He'd insist on them each using the toilet one last time for the night. If they needed anything more, they'd have to pee in the bushes. All the older kids were so excited. I think some of them actually had some weed back then. There were whispers about it," Stevie recalls.

"So your cousins were high?" Shelby asks.

"I didn't much give a crap. I was self-centered about my worries. Once everybody was out back, Uncle Bob would take us into the bathroom and force us to take that godawful green cough syrup by the dosage capful. We cried, but it did us no good. Then he'd help us all change into our pajamas, one by one, in the bathroom. Afterward, he helped us lay sleeping bags on the guest bedroom floor. The others always seemed to fall asleep first," Stevie remembers.

"Are you certain they were asleep or just pretending?" Shelby asks.

"Now I don't know, since I've learned the other knew something was going on. But Uncle Bob would make the bed up for himself while we slept on the floor. Then—"

"Stevie, I know this is difficult, but we need to get to the bottom of this," Shelby declares.

"I can't," Stevie bawls.

"Do you want to stop for today and talk about your OCD obsessions and compulsions and pick this discussion about Uncle Bob up on Thursday?" Shelby asks.

"Yes, please," Stevie blows her nose.

"Okay, how are you doing OCD-wise?" Shelby inquires.

"The swallowing is difficult. The coin rubbings, orderliness, and hair-pulling are still bothersome. Then there are observable behaviors to others, like sitting and standing repeatedly and shrugging my right shoulder to my right ear eight times," Stevie informs.

"And have you been doing some of the one nostril breathing or progressive body scan at any point?" Shelby wonders.

"No, it's difficult to relax with all this other stuff going on," Stevie says.

"But that's when you need them the most," Shelby notes.

"I'll make an effort to try harder to relax and do them," Stevie promises.

"Stevie, we can add an additional therapy session tomorrow morning at 7:00 am. I have that time slot open," Shelby suggests, "That might be for the best considering the extent of what we have to discuss."

"No," Stevie replies, "I need to go over in my mind what I need to get out. Please. Let's wait until Thursday's session."

"Okay, but Thursday's the day we bring the past into the present and deal with it, understand?"

16 Sin of Survival

"How did therapy go today?" Izzy asks Stevie outside of the school just after Morgan drops her daughter off curbside.

"Okay, I guess. I didn't accomplish what I needed to, but I still have Thursday, so no rush," Stevie reflects as their adversaries Godsey, Sway, and Zwirdle walk by, giggling, glancing, and whispering.

"Assholes," Stevie says, turning her back on them to hide her blinking.

"I thought the medicine was supposed to help with that," Nico says, approaching from the side.

"It's been helping with the majority of issues, except for the more extreme ones," Stevie surmises. "Like the stress of Godsey, Sway, and Zwirdle laughing at my expense while I'm trying to process this other crap in the background."

In no time, Stevie and Nico are in Biology, taking the final test of the year. The other students all glance over with curiosity at the eight different colored pens lined up at the ready on Stevie's desk. She continuously readjusts the paper in line with the front of the desk. The trio of adversaries is prodding Les to start another incident with Stevie, but he's not having it.

"If you want to piss her off, then go do it yourself," Les barks, and the trio settles down looking mighty peeved.

Later on, at lunch, Izzy, Nico, and Stevie gawked at the trio again. Sway, Godsey, and Zwirdle mock Stevie to the amusement of nearby friends until Elias walks in behind them and hears what they're saying.

"Skinny bitch can't drink a water bottle without choking, ack, gack, gack, ack," Zwirdle pokes fun at Stevie.

"Maybe skinny bitch should go postal on your weird-ass face. Hell, go to the bathroom and clean off that shit Zwirdle, you look like a fucking clown. The rest of your guys' makeup looks like shit, too. Dial it down a bit," Elias derides, which garners laughs from the onlookers.

"Elias, you really don't have to fight my battles for me. I'm fine."

"I hate this stigma shit. We shouldn't have to battle this with our disorder as well."

Elias, passing through the commons lunch area, continues on his way. After the fiery encounter, everyone returns to class, and all is well. After school, Mom is late picking up Stevie, who doesn't mind and just sits and hangs with Izzy and Nico. When Mom does drive up, she's wearing sunglasses, which isn't that uncommon, but it's a cloudy day. Stevie steps in and hears a random sniffle.

"Is anything up, Mom? Are you okay? You sound sick," Stevie asks.

"Your cousin, Kennedy, killed herself. It was by suicide," Mom reveals.

"Oh, my God, why?" Stevie spurts.

"There was a note, but I don't want to talk about it yet," Mom cries.

Stevie thinks back to her conversation with McKenna. Kennedy hovered about the room before she left. It was almost as if she wanted to say something to McKenna or Stevie.

"Holy crap," Stevie emits, then quickly turns to stare out the window, a lone tear streaming down her face.

Mom slams on the brakes and pounds her fists on the steering wheel. "Why this? Why now? Gram can't handle this news. Shit."

"What's wrong with Gram?"

"She's old and fragile and still getting over Pops' death," Mom says.

The rest of the day and the following one, Stevie spends deep cleaning the kitchen and pantry. Every cabinet and shelf is emptied, cleared of expired canned goods, wiped down, and reorganized to utter perfection. Late Wednesday night, around 10:50 pm, Stevie sprays down and disinfects the main floor powder room before she heads to her room for a shower.

Once in the shower, Stevie bawls and pounds on the shower tile. She slides to the shower floor, holding her knees tightly to her chest. The showerhead rains down on top of her until she's chilled and shivers. She slowly wipes down and dresses in her pajama shorts and tank top. The clock on the wall now reads: 1:12 am. Stevie pulls up her laptop on top of a pillow.

June 8th, 1:22 am
Basement Bedroom
Dear Journal,

What the fuck did I do? Could I have saved Kennedy's life if I'd come out and told my story first? Would that have saved her? Did she have nobody to speak to about it? Was she hovering because she wanted to talk to us about what happened?

I'm so stupid. I should've shared with Shelby and then told Mom and Dad the other day, right afterward. That would've been enough time to save a life.

How many of the older cousins has this happened to? Probably not many, or they'd have intervened to save us from all the shit.

Oh my God, what about McKenna, Josh, and Joey? Are they okay with all this happening? I hope they're not on the fence about self-harm.

And what did Mom mean when she said that Gram couldn't handle this? What about everyone else who has handled this? And we're still coping the best we can with all the discoveries that we don't even know the details.

<u>Plan of attack</u>
Tell Shelby
Tell Mom and Dad
Tell Gram

Oh, shit. I have to focus on McKenna first and let her know the timeline.

I think Mom knows something is up when I race out of the SUV and rush into the counseling center building, leaving Mom to amble on over to the coffee shop and spill tears in her teacup. All my attempts, by text, email, and phone, to McKenna have gone unanswered. I need to talk to Shelby NOW.

"Stevie, how are you today?" Shelby calls Stevie out of the waiting room. They rush back to her office in silence and sit down, ready to ramble.

"I messed up bad," Stevie spurts.

"How is that?" Shelby wonders.

"A cousin killed herself and left a note. I don't know what the note said, but I'm fairly positive that it involves what I need to share with you today," Stevie begins.

"Okay," Shelby takes a seat. "Is this in line with where we were headed on Tuesday?"

"Yes," Stevie gains composure and breathes deeply, and exhales.

"I'm ready when you are, Stevie," Shelby pulls her tablet into her lap.

For the remainder of the session, Stevie goes into detail about how Uncle Bob molested each of them: Stevie, McKenna, Josh, and Joey. And even though each of the young children woke up groggy and complaining of aches and pains, none of the adults thought anything out of the ordinary.

"It went on for years until Pops died, and Gram no longer felt like going to the casino for bingo," Stevie shares.

"So, do you want to bring your parents in here so we can talk about it, or will you be doing that at your home?" Shelby wonders.

"I don't think I have the guts to do it alone."

"When do you want to do this?" Shelby notes on her tablet?

"Next Tuesday, she's in your office."

"What will be the format? I can ask you questions, and you respond. You can talk the whole time, and I'll keep your parents from interrupting. A little of both?"

"My mom might not believe me," Stevie stews.

"And your dad?"

"I think my dad is waiting for me to come out and tell them," Stevie sputters.

"Good, he might help keep your mother on track and not go off on a tangent like worrying about your grandmother."

"Okay, well, our time is up, so I'd better go. I'll see you tonight in the group, Shelby."

"Maybe tell your parents when they're together that I'd like to see them in my office for a status update next Tuesday, okay?"

"Got it," Stevie replies, then walks down the hall. She walks past the coffee shop and taps on the window to get her mom's attention. Mom comes out and remains speechless all the way to Stevie's school.

Mom doesn't even inquire as to how my therapy session went. Does she know and just refuses to come to terms with it?

"Bye, Mom."

"Have a good day, Stevie."

Mom pulls off almost immediately after Stevie's feet touch the ground.

What the hell, Mom? Do you know? You wouldn't allow it to happen if you knew. Would you? Is this about protecting Gram or you? Dad doesn't know.

Or does he? What's the thing about I can tell him anything? He must suspect something. If so, why the hell would you allow your daughter to suffer with the knowledge and not want to take action?

The school day passes in a blur. Stevie attended everything expected of her, but she wasn't entirely present; her thoughts were elsewhere, which surprisingly made her OCD obsessions and compulsions less obvious at times.

To: Isadora Madsen
From: Stevie Mathews
CC: Nicolas Montgomery
Subject: therapy status

Hi, guys. I think it will be easier on me if I share this with you in the form of an email, and then we'll talk about it later. In therapy today, I shared my account of abuse at the hands of my Uncle Bob. He'd give my cousins and me, of similar age, green cough syrup that knocked us out, and then he'd molest us while the older cousins camped in a tent out back. And to add to the pain, one of those older cousins is the one who committed suicide the other day and left a note, which has my mother all riled up. That makes me wonder if she knows now or if she knew then? Keep this between us. No spoken words where others can hear. I love you guys.

Stevie signs off the computer in the library and makes certain nobody around her spies on her correspondence with her best friends. She feels better about getting it out in the open. Now she needs to contact McKenna.

To: Stevie Mathews
From: Nicolas Montgomery
CC: Isadora Madsen
Subject: Re: therapy status

Holy fucking shit. Are you okay? You did the right thing by bringing it out into the open. This is really heavy shit. I can't believe you've been carrying this around and haven't been able to tell anyone until now. You're so strong. I need to give you a hug if that's okay. I love you, and it hurts to know that you're in emotional pain because of some asshole. I'm here for you, Stevie.

Nico signs out and looks around to see if either of his best buddies is anywhere in sight.

To: Stevie Mathews
From: Isadora Madsen
CC: Nicolas Montgomery
Subject: Re: therapy status

Oh crap. That bastard. You're going to take this all the way and press charges, correct? He doesn't deserve to be around any kids, his own or anyone else's. I'm so sorry that you had to go through something like that. You've been through so much already with the OCD. Adding this to that must just be overwhelming. I love you, sweetie. I'm going to come looking for you now. I need to give you a hug. But I understand that it's too difficult to talk about, so we don't have to at this time. Nico and I are here for you.

Stevie is filling her backpack at her locker with all that remains after turning in her textbooks on the last day of school. It doesn't take long for her best buds to show up at their nearby lockers. Izzy drops her bag and goes to hug Stevie when Nico stands teary-eyed watching them. They wave him on in for a group hug.

"Okay, guys, I need to stop crying. I can't let on to Mom that anything unusual is happening," Stevie tells. "She's picking me up any minute."

"That's batshit crazy if she knows and is keeping it to herself," Izzy stammers.

"We're here for you, anytime. I'll sneak out in the middle of the night if you need me," Nico whispers.

The support of her friends helps get her through the day and evening until the OCD therapy group rolls around, and Dad takes Stevie to the counseling center.

"You've been very quiet today. Is everything okay?" Dad asks.

"At some point, it will be. Dad, I'm trying to work through some stuff right now. I forgot to tell Mom earlier, but Shelby would like both of you to join me in therapy on Tuesday. Is that okay?"

"Of course it is. I'll move my schedule around to make it happen. And I'll tell your mom when I get home so she can ask the Leingang's if they can watch Piper that morning. Sweetie, does this have anything to do with Kennedy's suicide?"

"I don't really want to get into that right now, Dad. Please respect my wishes," Stevie pleads.

"You do know that the funeral is on Saturday. We're all expected to attend. Are you up to that?"

"I guess that I'll have to be. Thank you, Dad, for understanding," Stevie walks off to the group.

17 Angels Also Die

Lucy waves Stevie over to sit next to her in the OCD therapy group meeting room. The seat on Stevie's other side is saved for Elias, who is using the restroom. Sally comes in and tries to take Elias's seat, but Lucy waves her off.

"No, I'm sitting there, Sally," Elias walks up from behind them.

Sally tries taking the seat on the other side of Lucy, but that one's saved for Henry, who has become friends with Lucy as of late.

"What's going on there?" Stevie smiles at Lucy.

"Nothing, really. We're not in a place for dating yet. We just really like that there's someone to talk to at 2:00 am when the rest of the world feels lost to us. Do you know what I mean?" Lucy says.

"I think so," Stevie responds.

"So, how has your week been?" Lucy wonders.

"Not great with a cousin dying by suicide. I didn't know her that well. It just makes you wish that you'd taken the time to talk with them more when they were here. Do you know what I mean?" Stevie explains. "She left a note. I don't know if that makes it better or worse because the survivors realize just how shitty of human beings we were to not pick up on the suffering."

"Listen to me, kiddo. You have an enormous heart. Don't ever wonder that you didn't do enough. I'm sure that you would've been there had you known. You can just sense that about some people."

"Thank you, Lucy."

Lucy picks up Stevie's hand and squeezes.

Shelby enters the room, and everyone standing takes a seat. "So, since we're all here from last week and there isn't anybody new this week, why don't we delve into some symptoms and ways to counter the compulsions. Who'd like to put themselves out there for the group?"

"Hello, everyone. Lucy here. I've had OCD since I was a teen, and I'm twenty-two now. I deal with horrific images, repeating routines with pathological slowness. Due to my meds, I've got anxiety and dizziness when standing up."

"What kind of horrific images," Ed asks.

"My dog died at the beginning of the year, right after the holidays. I was in shambles, and many days I still am. He was my therapy dog. He was a cavapoo, which is a mix of a Cavalier King Charles Spaniel and a poodle. The former is known for their heart problems, which is what he died of, and left me heartbroken and unable to stop the violent images blazing across my mind, some of which are of me hurting myself."

Stevie picks up Lucy's hand and squeezes.

"Okay, group, how do we counter the violent images?" Shelby asks.

"Metacognitive therapy, detached mindfulness, and observing one's thoughts," Marvin suggests.

"Tell us about that, Marvin," Shelby nudges.

"Well, it's kind of like viewing yourself viewing those images. Observe yourself thinking, almost like a lab rat, I say. That way, you can see how illogical those images are or if you need to get more help with something. Further care if you truly are in danger of hurting yourself. We love you, Lucy," Marvin finishes.

"Good to note, Marvin. Thank you. Any other suggestions for these symptoms?"

"Distraction techniques such as the ABCs of cities, states, or countries like Atlanta, Boston, Canada," Elias shares. "Or names of fruits like apple, blueberry, cherry, things like that."

"How about lists of five, like call to mind five musicians, or books, or things in your purse, or blue things in the room?" Ed offers.

"Lucy, do you plan on hurting yourself?" Shelby asks.

"No, I just need help to keep the images at bay," Lucy specifies. "No need for the psych ward here. The images are of a distant me. Everyone, I'm fine.

"Okay. Lucy, just see me after group, okay?" Shelby prods. "Anybody else want to share symptoms?"

"I have similar images, but more of a phobia than hurting myself. I should be happy because I'm graduating high school tomorrow, but instead, I walk around with the image of my birth mother entering my front door and emptying a bucket of snakes that all slither towards me, hissing."

How about the three keys to facing one's fears being repetition, frequency, and prolonged time?" Henry suggests. "Or positive self-talk?"

"Henry, care to explain?" Shelby asks.

"Bring the thought to mind, repeatedly of your own accord, not just when it shows up on its own, and spend time with the thought. Check out what else is happening in the room, be present with it until it holds no bounty over you," Henry expounds.

The last part of the group is dedicated to a

body scan, which is led by Lucy, who is all giggles. After class, Shelby does the obligatory check-in with Lucy to make certain all is well and that no self-injury will occur. Lucy, Elias, and Henry wait for her, then walk over to the coffee shop together and sit down for a chat. When they enter the coffee shop, Sally waves Stevie over, saying she saved her a seat, but Stevie respectfully declines, and instead, Shelby sits with Sally.

Over the course of the hour, Stevie, Lucy, Henry, and Elias have a boisterous discussion on distraction techniques like lists of awesome action-adventure moves and sappy romantic comedies. The table often erupts with laughter. Stevie is grateful she fell in with such an incredible group. In the end, the guys shake hands, and Stevie and Lucy hug. Group members wish Zoey Congratulations on her graduation, and everybody goes their own way.

"Stevie, don't get stressed, but Mom is frantic over the fact that Shelby wants to see us in your therapy session on Tuesday. Don't let it deter you. Do you understand?" Dad says when Stevie climbs into the truck after the fellowship at the coffee shop ends.

"Is she mad at me?" Stevie asks Dad.

"If anything, she's mad at Shelby," Dad clarifies.

"Shelby's just helping me," Stevie relays.

"Mom is all over the place with fear right now—fear for you, fear for Gram, fear for the family," Dad shares. "Just give her some space until Tuesday. Okay."

"Okay, Dad," Shelby reveals. "I feel like I'm

doing something wrong."

Dad slams on the brakes and takes Stevie's hand in his. "Don't you feel like any of this is your fault? It's not. I just need you to work on your OCD and anything else that may be bothering you. Don't let anybody stand in the way of your recovery. Promise me that you'll do that," Dad asks.

Mom spends the next day in bed with a headache while Stevie cleans the house: vacuuming, using the wet duster, wiping down all the surfaces, and facing anything and everything forward, such as knick-knacks, picture frames, candles, and ambient lighting. She rearranges her bedroom, makeup vanity, and bathroom cabinets. Stevie even does the windows before making a casserole for dinner.

On Saturday, Stevie's family readies itself for the three-and-a-half-hour road trip up north to the town where the family cabin is located. Kennedy will be buried in a family lot in the small summer resort town, which is bustling with cabin goers, day fishermen, and city-dwellers road-tripping and spending the day at a local beach.

It feels weird—so much happiness in the air. Laughter from little kids, giggles from teenagers crossing the street to the general store, adults are going antique shopping, or elderly people walking from the retirement home to the museum or library. What about Kennedy? She's dead for Chrissakes. Don't all these people care that such a young life is gone? Who the hell is calling me? I don't know this number. I'm at a funeral. I'm grieving the loss of someone in a lot of pain. Oh, there's McKenna.

When she glances at Stevie, McKenna's mother grabs her daughter's hand and pulls her in the opposite direction. Then a text comes in from the same random number. It reads: Are you Lucy's friend? Family members are looking at Stevie fiddling with her phone at the funeral. It vibrates. One last look, and it's Elias calling. She quickly texts back: Not now!

I can't believe this. He knows I'm at a funeral. How inappropriate of him. Are you Lucy's friend? What the hell is that? Lucy knows I'm at this funeral, too. If she knew someone was bothering me in her name, she'd kill—

Stevie turns and walks to the back of the gathering for a second and pulls out her phone. She can almost sense the following text that she is about to read: Lucy is dead. Stevie returns the phone to her pocket and walks back to sit with her parents and Piper. She's bombarded with thoughts and begins blinking. Dad pulls Piper between him and Mom, then takes Stevie's hand with his other hand. She begins raising her right shoulder to her right ear. With her left hand, she wipes a stray tear.

After all is said and done at the church and cemetery, the entire family meets at the family cabin, which is rather large considering the additions built onto it to sleep twenty-two people, most of which are bunk, trundle, or Murphy beds. Then there's always floor space for a sleeping bag when the weather is too wicked for the tents out back.

"Stevie, are you okay?" Dad whispers.

"A friend from the OCD group just died, too," Stevie murmurs back, causing Dad to hug her.

There's food out everywhere, but the only people eating are the younger family members. Kennedy's mom bawls as she hugs everyone who stops by her to give condolences. Kennedy's dad and her teenage boyfriend sniffle and wipe their eyes. Out of the corner of her eye, she spies McKenna whispering to Josh and Joey. Stevie makes her way over towards them when McKenna turns and nods her head to the door. Stevie follows her out and back into the woods, separating the cabin from the nearest neighbors.

"So, what's going to happen with you?" McKenna asks Stevie.

"I talked to my therapist and told her everything. So on Tuesday, my parents will join me in my therapy session where I'll reveal what happened to them," Stevie says.

"So, what happens then?" McKenna wonders.

"What do you mean?"

"Are you going to tell about my brothers and me, too?"

"Yes," Stevie spurts.

"What time on Tuesday?"

"7:00 am, so we'll be done at 7:50 in case you're wondering when the fallout could be," Stevie informs.

"You don't plan on hurting yourself, do you?" McKenna asks.

"No, you?"

"No."

"What do you want to come of this?"

"I don't know," McKenna replies. "You?"

"I want him to get help and be kept away from children for the rest of his life," Stevie continues, "I am worried about Gram and how she'll take it."

"Will you chicken out?" McKenna wonders.

"Not a chance. I need to do this for myself. My road to recovery has all these extra obstacles on it right now. I need to do this for my sanity," Stevie explains.

McKenna hugs Stevie, and they part ways. Stevie looks up to one of the parents' bedroom windows and sees her mother watching her. Stevie turns around, but McKenna is nowhere to be seen. She turns back up to the window, but her mother is no longer there either.

It's a long, quiet ride home. Piper attempts to play car games, but nobody is up for it. She falls asleep after a short while, only to wake after Dad stops at the rest stop. Everyone but Mom goes to the restroom. Stevie's finished first but waits for Piper, but mainly Dad.

I can't go back in that car with her alone. The tension is excruciating. I know she knows. She knows I know she knows. Wouldn't the motherly thing be to talk about it as a family? And Lucy? Oh my God, what happened? Was it suicide? I'd think Elias would've detailed more if it had been a car accident. Did she leave a letter?

"Stevie, are you okay?" Dad asks when he exits the rest area.

"Yeah, Dad, thanks."

"What's wrong with Stevie?" Piper asks.

"Nothing, Piper."

"Then why didn't you ask if I'm okay?" Piper pouts.

"Piper, are you okay?" Dad asks. Both Dad and Stevie roll their eyes at each other and smile.

Once they arrive home, they all shower and change. Dad leaves Mom in the bedroom to nap while he and Piper play board games on the living room floor. Stevie texts Henry and Elias but doesn't get a response from either. She sits on the edge of her bed and pulls on her hair to get it to look right.

Stevie lies down and screams into her pillow, then just lies there, eyes glossed over, until she falls asleep. Hours later, the clock on the nightstand reads 9:26 pm. Stevie's phone vibrates.

"Hello?" Stevie answers.

"Hi, Stevie? It's Henry."

"Oh my God, Henry. I couldn't answer at first because I was at a funeral, but then I tried and tried, and neither you nor Elias picked up."

"I'm sorry. I had two back-to-back appointments with clients, one of which was a working business dinner that ran late."

"So, what happened to Lucy?"

"We were supposed to go for a run along the bluff overlooking the flood plains. So I went to her townhouse, and she wasn't answering the door. I called her to no avail. So, I tried the front door, and it was open. She was up in her bedroom, lying on the bed with a glass of wine, and tipped over a bottle of pills on the nightstand. They were sedatives. I have no idea how much she took. I checked to see if she was alive. By her pallor, I knew she wasn't. So I called the police, they interviewed me, and I left a message on Shelby and Elias's phone. I got your number off her phone and tried it, but I couldn't get hold of you," Henry elaborates.

"Any suicide note?" Stevie asks.

"I didn't see one out in the open. I don't know because I never really looked around the place. I left as soon as they let me," Henry sniffles. "I just think that she seemed so happy the other night that I can't imagine her taking her own life.

"I know. Thank you for taking my call, Henry. I really appreciate it. I'm going to go now. Bye," Stevie cries.

18 The Day the World Fell

Stevie all but gets off the phone with Henry when a voice-to-text comes in from Elias:

Stevie, I'm sorry. Today was too much for me. I can't do this. I care about you, so I don't want to hurt you, but I just can't handle a serious relationship right now. I'm sorry about your cousin's death and Lucy's death. I know this must be very difficult for you, but I'm just not mature enough to handle all this heavy shit.

"You're a year older than me, you dumb little shit," Stevie stammers. She tosses her phone aside and screams into her pillow.

To: Isadora Madsen
From: Stevie Mathews
CC: Nicolas Montgomery
Subject: life and death

Hi, guys. I'm sorry if my subject line is a little dramatic. I just feel like crap and need to vent out into the universe. I don't want to talk right now. I'm tired of talking. Life sucks. No, I'm not going to commit suicide, or anything like that, so don't come rushing over or call my parents. I just want to scream to someone that life is hard on me, too, and I'm still here. This OCD shit has taken a toll on me this year, and now a funeral for my cousin on the same day as the death of an OCD group member that I got close to; and to top it all off, Elias breaks up with me because he thinks that he's too immature for this shit. The stupid asshole is a coward. Grr. Life sucks today. I'm just venting. Thanks for being there for me, guys. I love you. Goodnight.

Stevie tosses the laptop aside and leans back against the tufted headboard. Time passes on the nightstand clock: 10:01 pm, 10:44 pm, 11:30 pm.

To: Stevie Mathews
From: Nicolas Montgomery
CC: Isadora Madsen
Subject: Re: life and death

Call me anytime. I'm up. I don't know what to say besides Elias is an asshole and that you're strong and can get through this. You don't have to do it alone, Stevie. We're here for you.

Stevie blows her nose and carries the tissue like it's a toxic substance to the toilet. She then sprays down the handle and lid as if they were contaminated. Stevie's computer dings.

To: Stevie Mathews
From: Isadora Madsen
CC: Nicolas Montgomery
Subject: Re: life and death

Nico said it well. I'm babysitting some little

cousins having a birthday sleepover with my little sister, but if you want to talk, then I'll make myself available. Stevie, you're loved, and you've got support ready to bolster you up. Elias is a jerk. Not everybody is like that. I know that you really liked him, but he's an asshole. You don't need him because you got us. I love you.

The next two days are mind-numbing, waiting for time to pass. Tuesday is therapy day with Stevie's parents and Shelby. And though she looks forward to Thursdays, it's the day of Lucy's funeral. Then there's the group that will be nothing like it was before. Stevie is considering not even attending.

"Mr. and Mrs. Mathews, Stevie, it's good to see you," Shelby greets them in the waiting room. "I'm so sorry about the loss of Lucy. She'll be missed. We can discuss this further later."

Once in the room, Stevie sits by the window nearest Shelby's desk. Dad takes up roost on the chair opposite the end table from Stevie, while Mom sits on the loveseat in the corner near the door. Dad leans forward with his elbows on his knees, ready to get down to brass tacks.

"Well, I called you here today to discuss things that came up in therapy."

"Did they arise in therapy, or are these planted memories?" Mom spills.

"You don't even know what I'm going to tell you, do you, Mrs. Mathews?"

"One can only imagine," Mom blurts.

"Morgan, this is for our daughter. We're here to help in any way we can to make things better for her. For Chrissakes, Kennedy just killed herself. We don't want that for Stevie, damn it."

"Mrs. Mathews, please understand, nobody wants to unfurl this history, but it's necessary for recovery and growth," Shelby says. "Stevie has something to say. Let's listen to her."

"Dad, Mom, back when we stayed overnights at Gram's and Pop's place, when all the parents would go to the casino. Uncle Bob would send the older kids out back to camp lakeside, while McKenna, Josh, Joey, and I slept in the guest bedroom." Stevie pauses because Mom has tears streaming down her face.

"Stevie, continue," Shelby says to Stevie while Dad leans forward and puts his face into his hands.

"Uncle Bob gave us that green cough syrup that made us really sleepy, but sometimes we didn't fall asleep fast, and we were awake when he—"

"Stop, I can imagine it, okay? You don't have to go into details. I've already read the suicide notes Kennedy left. I know what Bob did," Mom disintegrates into tears.

"What? What the hell, Morgan? You knew about this." Dad steams. "Why didn't you share this with me?" Dad stands up and puts his hands on his hips and bellows, "You knew that I'd kick his ass at the funeral, didn't you? That son-of-a-bitch."

"I thought he stopped. We thought he grew out of it," Mom sputters. "My sisters and I thought it was a one-time thing when we were younger. He apologized, and it never happened again. We didn't want to hurt Gram, so we never spoke of it."

"What the fuck?" Dad blurts.

"When my sister noticed the cough syrup out

one morning after a casino concert, and the kids seemed groggy, we agreed the sleepovers were worth the chance that it could happen to them," Mom reveals.

"You let our daughter stay with a pedophile?"

"He's my brother," Mom whispers.

"I don't care that he's your brother. We're pressing charges," Dad fumes. "And not only that. I'm going to kick his ass."

"Mr. and Mrs. Mathews, I will have to report this sexual abuse at the hands of Stevie's Uncle Bob," Shelby informs.

"I know. I've already warned my sisters about this therapy session. I think they're expecting to talk to their kids about it today, too," Mom says, still wiping tears.

"I'm really disappointed in you, Morgan. I'm your husband, and you've been discussing this with your sisters and not your daughter or me," Dad cries. "I've been sick to my stomach for days, wondering what Stevie would say today, imagining the worst, and I undershot it tenfold because my wife already knew that our daughter had been molested because she, in fact, had been, too, and allowed the perpetrator to do it again."

"Liam?" Mom whispers through tears.

"I can't even look at you right now, Morgan." Dad wipes his face with both hands, then wrings them out and sighs deeply. "Stevie, I'm so sorry. What can I do for you?"

"I just needed to tell you. I had to release it. Believe me when I say that I don't want to cause anyone any pain. McKenna and I just needed to get things out in the open. She's worried about Josh and

Joey, who are in therapy, but it doesn't seem like things are going well for them. We worry about another suicide."

Dad gestures to Stevie to stand up, and he hugs her, all the while weeping like a baby. "Is there anything else you want to tell us?"

"I'm sorry that it happened, and I'm sorry Gram will be devastated. I don't mean to bring pain to our family, especially after Kennedy's death. I feel ashamed," Stevie spiels.

Dad holds Stevie at arm's length, "You have absolutely nothing to be ashamed of, Stevie. Do you understand? There is no way in hell that this was your fault. You don't have to worry. It will all be handled appropriately from here on out."

"Mom, I'm sorry. I love you," Stevie cries.

Mom bawls. She doesn't look anyone in the eye. Instead, she gets up and leaves Dad and Stevie behind to discuss the fallout with Shelby. Mom disappears into the restroom.

"I can't believe she left. She can't get anywhere because I've got the keys. Shelby, what's going to happen now?" Dad wonders. He and Stevie return to their seats.

"I'm going to notify the proper authorities. You'll probably get a visit from a detective who will ask you all the same things we just discussed and wants to know more details. Then he'll take names and interview McKenna, Josh, and Joey. Even if the other three say nothing, there is already enough here with Stevie's account. Uncle Bob will be arrested, and the courts will take it from there. If you want to warn anybody about the police visits like McKenna, Josh, or Joey, or their parents, you might want to do so as soon as possible so that they're not blindsided."

"Okay," Dad nods.

"Stevie, I want to thank you for sharing those disturbing events with us. I can only imagine how difficult it was for you to do so," Shelby says.

"Oh, God, yes, Stevie, you did an incredible job. You're so brave. Forget about Mom for the time being. I think that she's going through some of her own memories as well. I'm not releasing her from the fact that she knew and didn't prevent this from happening to you kids, but let's just give this time. You continue to talk to Shelby and do your group. Your mother and I will work this out somehow, someway, in a matter of time," Dad tells. "I'm going to use the restroom, then find your mother. I'll meet you out by the car if you want to finish up with Shelby in here. Thanks, Shelby."

After Dad leaves, Stevie turns to Shelby and says, "Believe it or not, I think that went better than I imagined. I was half scared to death."

"Well, just know that you've got support behind you. I know Lucy's gone, and there's that to deal with, too; but you've got Elias and the rest of us in the group, and you've got other friends, correct?"

"Elias broke up with me. He said it was too much for him to handle at this time," Stevie wipes a tear from her eye, "But that's okay because I've got two incredible best friends who stand by me through thick and thin."

"Stevie, I'm so sorry that you have all this on your plate. Ugh. Elias!" Shelby grumbles and shakes her head. "Please don't back out of the group. I think it is really beneficial for you. There's that other girl in there your age, Zoey. Maybe sit by her, or me, or there's always Sally." Shelby and Stevie both laugh through tears.

Scrubbing the tile grout, dusting like there's no tomorrow, cleaning out the fridge and oven, and wiping down the appliances and walls fill the next day and a half for Stevie.

"Stevie, are you ready?" Dad yells down the stairwell to the basement.

"Are you going to the funeral, too, Dad?" Piper asks.

"Yes, I am, sweetie."

"Did you know Stevie's friend?"

"No, I didn't, but I'm here to show support for Stevie."

"Shall I go, too?" Piper focuses. "I want to help Stevie."

Dad glances over into the kitchen, where Mom pours a glass of wine and flips through pages in a magazine. Mom looks away.

"No, honey. Thank you for offering, though. That alone says a lot," Dad glares in Mom's direction.

"Stevie, we're going to be late," Dad shouts.

After Stevie strokes the feng shui coins attached to the red ribbon affixed to the trim on the front entry door, she takes a seat on the passenger's side of the truck.

"Are you prepared for this?" Dad asks.

"How do you prepare for a funeral?" Stevie says.

"Is Elias meeting you there?"

"I don't know what Elias is doing," Stevie

snaps.

"Did you have a disagreement?"

"Yeah, I wanted to be an adult, and he'd rather remain an immature kid," Stevie spews.

"May I ask what happened?"

"He broke up with me because things have been getting too heavy, and he can't deal with it," Stevie relays.

"That little shit. May I have a word with him?" Dad begs.

"No. Dad. I mean it. I can fight my own battles. And if he wants to be a jerk, then so be it. Leave him alone." Once they arrive, Stevie stays stuck in her own mind.

The funeral is smaller than Kennedy's. Lucy has more friends than family. What does that say about a person? It's an open casket. She looks so peaceful. Damn it, Lucy. What did you do? Why? I really could benefit from our friendship. Why didn't you reach out to me? Or was it just some unlucky accident? Lucy? Oh, shit. I'm crying already. Wow. Dad had a tissue. We could always count on Mom for that, but like everything else lately, I don't know where Mom is emotionally, mentally. She's been talking to her sisters a lot, especially after the detectives interviewed me and recorded me. I'd like to think that she doesn't blame me for anything, but who the hell knows? Oh, there's that asshole Elias with Henry. It appears they came together. And here are Marvin and Ed. Oh, and Shelby is up closer to the front. I want to run and hide…from life. Is that what happened, Lucy? Did you want to run and hide from life?

The funeral is successful in that Stevie avoids Elias. That's a good thing because she seems uncertain about whether she wants to scream, cry at, or beat him. Dad sure gave him looks, though. Elias kept looking at Stevie, but when he realized Mr. Mathews was watching him, Elias turned away.

June 15th, 4:30 pm
Basement Bedroom
Dear Journal,

Why do some people have all the luck? Two funerals within a week, not to mention a break-up and disclosing childhood molestation at the hands of a trusted family member. Oh, and where's Mom? I don't mean physically. We all live in this same house where pretty much only three of us are talking.

I sensed Elias staring at me at the funeral. I think Dad caught him, too. I bet if looks could kill. Henry looked as if he wanted to come and speak to me, but he was protecting his little buddy: the little shit.

Izzy and Nico are there for me around the clock with texts, emails, and phone calls. It's good to have friends, especially when family can't be there for you.

At first, I hated Shelby for putting me in the hospital, but I see now that she had to prevent me from turning out like Lucy or, worse, hurting my family. Anyhow, Shelby has come through for me lately. Shelby gave me a hug after the funeral and said that she hoped she'd see me tonight in the group, but realized how difficult things are for me right now.

Ugh. Shall I go? Or shall I stay?

Elias, you little shit, I want to yell at your face.

I've been through more difficult things this week. So I'm not going to let a little rat bastard get the better of me and prevent me from enjoying the group. I'm going.

19 Once Upon and Apology

"I'm sorry, Stevie. Please forgive me?" Elias says from where he stands behind Stevie at the water fountain off the lobby of the counseling center. They're waiting for the doors to be unlocked and the group welcomed in to be seated.

Stevie turns around and glares at Elias.

"I know I was an asshole. I got scared. Lucy's death made it all so real for me. I thought you'd be next, and I didn't think I could handle being so close to you, and then you'd die," Elias's eyebrows and nose are red, and his cheeks are flushed while tears well up in his eyes.

Shelby exits the elevator in a rush and bumps into Stevie. "Are you okay, Stevie?"

Stevie nods.

"Elias?" Shelby asks.

"No, I made an ass out of myself, and I'm begging for forgiveness," Elias stumbles.

"Oh, I see," Shelby pauses. "Well, it's time for the group."

Stevie steps between Elias and Shelby and walks over to the double-entry doors to the conference room. Shelby follows and unlocks the room. The group finds stacking chairs against the wall and makes a circle. Stevie chooses to sit next to Zoey on one side and Sally on the other. Elias sits next to Marvin and Henry.

"Tonight, we are short a few people. But first things first: we need to address a major happening in our group; Lucy, who normally sits over there by the doors, has passed away. We don't know the specifics, just that her funeral was today, and a few of us from this group attended after being notified of her passing," Shelby informs.

"Oh, my God, no," Sally spurts.

"Why don't we go around the room and take turns sharing something you remember about her, something she said or did that we can all remember her by on this sad evening," Shelby encourages. "I'll start. Lucy made me laugh. And I saw how she brought laughter to others. She had a powerful spirit."

"I met Shelby in the hospital. She was focused on her battle with OCD. She really tried hard to get over the obsessions and compulsions. And you're right. She was funny," Marvin says.

"She shared a smoke with me a few times. She was trying to quit, but had been a little anxious with her new drugs making her dizzy. She worried about having to give up her license if the dizziness worsened," Ed reveals.

Sally says, "She always included me even though I felt like I was intruding. I admired her go-get-em attitude. She was a lovely young lady."

Stevie clears her throat, "Lucy was a confidant that I only met a few weeks ago. It was easy to grow close to her so quickly. She nudged me when I hesitated and supported me when I was scared. I really miss her."

"Did you go to her funeral?" Sally asks.

Stevie nods. Zoey pats Stevie's leg.

"I didn't really know her. We didn't really talk. I remember last week when she said she had horrific images; some of them showed her harming herself. It's scary to think that any one of us can be on the verge of doing something irreversible. She did have a big spirit and lit up her side of the room," Zoey shares.

Henry says, "Lucy was a workout buddy as of recent. She was quite the cheerleader for recovery." Henry clears his throat. "Lucy was a beautiful person inside and out.

"Lucy helped me ask out the girl of my dreams," Elias says. "She confronted me when I was being shy or a little shit. Lucy wasn't afraid to put you in your spot if you were out of line, and she didn't shy away from helping a suffering soul. I wish she were still here. I need her this evening."

"Okay, why don't we share some of the necessities required to deal with obsessive-compulsive disorder?. What do we need?" Shelby asks.

Marvin says, "Sleeping well. We need to be well-rested to be strong enough to battle our thoughts and fears and resist our compulsions."

"Eating well is high in my book because I can tell when I eat crap like doughnuts and sugary juices that I don't feel as good when I eat like fruits or vegetables, or even a salad," Ed shares.

"Workouts. Exercise is important. In fact, Lucy and I were running buddies. The morning I found her, we were actually supposed to be cross-country running on the bluffs above the flood plains."

"Oh, my God, Henry. You were the one who found her?" Sally shrieks.

But on that note about workouts, the opposite is true; we need to relax. We need to set aside time to decompress and take a load off. Because when we're stressed, the symptoms deflate us tenfold," Marvin says.

"Meditation, like yoga, is helpful, I think," Zoey adds.

Shelby asks, "Why do you think?"

"Because we become one with the moment and stretch and hold it to truly be with our bodies."

"Excellent," Shelby responds to Zoey.

"Therapy is necessary. I've found, especially this last week, that it is life-altering. We need to get the thoughts out of our minds and share them with someone who can help us deal with our feelings. I didn't use to feel that way, especially in the hospital, where it felt like people were out to get me. But I now know the counseling was only there to help me," Stevie says.

"And medication. We can't go off of that on our own accord. I tried it and failed miserably. It works on the chemicals in our brain to help right our minds so we can achieve our better selves," Elias shares.

"Good, why don't we spend the rest of our time doing the full-body scan?" Shelby suggests and leads the group.

Afterward, Elias reaches for Stevie's hand and asks to talk to her alone. "Look, I was an ass. I see that now. It was just a gut reaction."

"It was a gut reaction to be an ass? That doesn't make me want to get to know you further," Stevie says.

"I'm sorry. That's all I can say. I pray to God it is enough. I can't lose you, Stevie." Elias pleads.

"I do not promise anything beyond just friends. Your words and actions really hurt me. I wanted to scream at you," Stevie reveals.

"Go ahead. Yell at me. I deserve it."

"You're an ass. The only reason I'm letting you back into my life is because of Lucy. She was a live-for-today, forget about what's expected of us, and do what we feel we need," Stevie tells.

"Can I buy you a mocha Frappuccino?" Elias asks.

"I suppose so. How's Henry doing?" Stevie inquires.

"I don't know. I didn't ask. I figured he wanted to deal with it on his own," Elias responds.

"You really are an ass. Let's go to the coffee shop and see Henry?"

"Hey, Henry. How are you?" Stevie gives him a big hug. Then they sit back down next to Marvin, who's talking about hoarding and fixed bedtime rituals to ward off evil.

"So, didn't you say you were going to hire a professional organizer to get you back to square one and go from there?" Henry asks.

"Well, ideally, that's what I want to do, but I don't think that I can give up that much control over my home. It's an organized mess where I know where everything is. Could any of you really allow someone to go into your space and reorganize?" Marvin asks.

"No, I couldn't," Henry says. "Just the thought of talking to new people has me on edge. Lately, I've worried about going crazy or blind so much so that I repeat sentences I already spoke to myself. Lucy's death made it worse. I fear that if she was that close to death and seemed like she had it all together, then I must be really fucked up and don't stand a chance," Henry blinks while scratching his forehead.

They continue sharing other obsessions and compulsions, and share how Lucy would've made the chat more worthwhile. As 10:00 pm rolls around, Stevie eyes her mom sitting out in her SUV in the parking lot, presumably waiting for Stevie, which makes her feel nauseous. Elias walks Stevie outside and mingles their fingers. But Stevie holds her own and pulls away first. They wave goodnight, and Stevie climbs into her mom's SUV.

"I'm probably the last person you wanted to see tonight, but I thought we needed to talk, so I asked your dad if I could pick you up instead. Is that okay with you?" Mom asks.

"Yeah, sure," Stevie responds.

"I thought your dad said that the boy broke up with you?"

"He apologized for being an ass."

"I guess I can't throw shade considering my behavior this past week," Mom says.

"Are you reading up on teenage lingo again?"

"Nevertheless, I'm glad that he apologized to you for treating you the way he did. And now for my apology," Mom shrieks. "I'm so sorry for letting you stay with Uncle Bob. But in my defense, we thought what he did to us girls was an isolated event and that he'd never ever hurt one of you kids, let alone five of you."

"I'm sorry that he hurt you, too. It must have been very painful to carry that with you all your life. I think it was painful for me, so I blocked it out.

And then the questions about the color aversions triggered something in me that spilled over once touched upon in therapy."

"I should've been a better mother back then on those casino nights and then again this past week when you were experiencing so much pain."

Stevie hugs her mom tight.

"When I think back, I remember you being groggy in the morning once. That's when your uncle said you'd been coughing, so he gave you baby cough syrup. Then there was another time when it happened to McKenna, but I never put two and two together. I'm so sorry, Stevie."

"What did he do to you when you were little?"

"One night we were playing in the liquor cabinet while Gram and Pop were out with friends, and we pretty much don't remember most of the night as it was hard liquor, but I remember him being on top of me, and I screamed, but my sisters were asleep, or should I say knocked out. Then he did the same thing to them, and they were only mildly cognizant of what was happening?"

"Did you ever talk to him about it?"

"Yes, we confronted him. He said the liquor made him do it. We believed him because the liquor made us susceptible to it. It was just the perfect storm. But we didn't want to hurt Gram and Pop because Pop had started having his heart condition around then, and Gram was so worried. We didn't want to lose either of them for something some stupid kids did that was or wasn't our fault."

"Mom, what were you thinking when you saw me out in the woods talking to McKenna?"

"I worried about Gram. I felt like our lives were just going to come crashing down upon us. It was like impending doom. It scared me half to death. I didn't know what we were going to do when you came out and told the police."

"And now, Mom? What do you think, now?"

"Now, I worry that you won't forgive me for my lapse in judgment. I'm your mother first and foremost. You are my love, my enjoyment, my happiness, my responsibility, my present, and my future. Gram will get through it just fine. And Uncle Bob needs to get help in addition to paying for what he's done."

"Everybody's left the parking lot except the coffee shop staff, who are cleaning up and ready to close it down for the night. Maybe we should get on home now, Mom?"

Once home, Dad is awake in the living room. Piper went to bed a long time ago. Dad approaches Mom and Stevie. "How did it go?"

"We're good, Dad," Stevie says.

"Stevie, make no mistake about it. Uncle Bob is going to pay for what he did to you kids. Don't waste any guilt on the man. And don't worry about Gram. She's shocked and angry as we are. Yes, he's her son, but she loves you, children, dearly."

"Thanks, Dad."

"Stevie, you need to take your medicine before you go to bed."

"Okay, Mom." Stevie follows Mom into the kitchen for the medicine and some juice. Afterward, she kisses and hugs her parents goodnight.

To: Isadora Madsen

From: Stevie Mathews
CC: Nicolas Montgomery
Subject: emotional status

Okay, Elias and I are going to be friends and we'll see where it goes. I'm still heartbroken over losing my OCD group friend, Lucy. There's an emptiness in the group without her. It's time for me to focus on bettering my health, now, though. My obsessions and compulsions have been rough this past week. So I need to be a little self-centered and do what's best for me. Does that sound arrogant or ignorant? Oh, well, you gotta do what you gotta do to get up in the morning and pull yourself up by your bootstraps. For now, goodnight. And I love you, guys, immensely.

Stevie sets her laptop down on the bed and goes in to take a shower. She's not strong enough to ward off the evil compulsions like cleaning grout with the toothbrush or spraying down the mirror eight times.

To: Stevie Mathews
From: Nicolas Montgomery
CC: Isadora Madsen
Subject: Re: emotional status

Good for you, Stevie. We're here to support you. I'm glad Elias is back, albeit as a friend. He's a nice guy. I think he just got scared and faltered. But if it came down to it, I'd be on your side, no questions asked. I love you, guys.

Stevie combs out her wet hair and tries to get it to lay perfectly as it dries. When she can't, she makes fists and yanks until her computer distracts.

To: Stevie Mathews
From: Isadora Madsen
CC: Nicolas Montgomery
Subject: Re: emotional status

I don't know about Elias. I'm not too keen on forgiving him for being an ass. How did the group go? Without Lucy? Is your mom still being an ass, too? Apologies are a dime a dozen; follow through with sincerity is key.

20 Cries of Existence

Stevie vacuums her bedroom, moving all the furniture. Something seems out of place to her. She organizes her quilting station, laying each spool of thread meticulously. She folds and refolds her fat quarters and other fabric remnants.

After hearing a noise outside, she pulls open the mini-blinds and spots a speck of dust. So she goes into the bathroom and opens a new package of toothbrushes. She returns to the window to resume cleaning the mini blinds one row at a time. Then there are the tracks of the window frame. With the lights on in her bedroom and the darkness outside, Stevie catches her reflection in the window and cries. She finishes up and sniffs her clothes. They smell like chemicals. She undresses on her way to the bathroom, where she climbs into the shower again and uses the squeegee to clean the shower door.

June 16th, 3:11 am
Basement Bedroom
Dear Journal,

Why can't I get through this fucking disorder? I mean, I've learned some techniques to master obsessions and compulsions.

Meditation and yoga help.
I eat well, not a fanatic, but not much sugar or carbs.
I could exercise more, maybe start to run.

What other suggestions have I followed?

Therapy truly has turned things around for me. I wasn't kidding tonight in group therapy when I said that it is life-altering. I couldn't have disclosed the molestation to Shelby. Plus, I needed someone who knew Elias to vent to about the break-up.

Medication. Hmm. Maybe it's time to ask for a change-up.

Things I need to work on would be sleeping well. I've got this penchant for late-night cleaning and journaling about my cleaning or making lists. Plus, during the school year, overnights are my go-to for assignments. I can think better when the house is quiet.

But with the one nostril breathing, lower diaphragmatic breathing, and the body scan, along with mental lists, I should be good to go, but when the tension arises, I get lost in it.

Lucy, if you're listening. I miss you.

The following morning finds Stevie overtired and antsy. Mom and Dad had meetings with colleagues and clients downtown. Stevie will also be watching Piper while Mom attends her first psychiatric appointment, where she's going to request a therapist at the counseling center to work through details of the past week, in addition to decades ago with her brother.

"Where's Mom?" Piper asks while getting a bowl of cereal and sitting opposite Stevie at the kitchen table.

"Work stuff."

"All day?"

"Most of it."

"What am I supposed to do?"

"Let me do your hair, Piper."

"No, thank you. I'll find something to do on my own."

"Why not, Piper?"

"Stevie, you always go overboard. Plus, I don't want you to hurt me. I see how you tug on your hair."

"Piper, I'd never hurt you."

"No, thank you."

"Do you want to go over to Izzy's and swim in her pool?"

"Sure. That'll be fun. I like Izzy."

"When?"

"I'll check with her, but around lunchtime?"

"You're not supposed to eat and swim. My teacher told us that. I'm serious."

"I didn't say we were going to eat and swim, Piper. I said around that time then we could get something to eat afterward. We can ride our bikes over to the fast-food restaurants."

"Ride when we're all wet? No, thanks."

"We'd take a change of clothes and use her hairdryer. Do I have to spell it out for you, Piper?"

"Will you be this cranky the entire time?"

"Piper?"

"What about Elias?"

"What about him?"

"He's cute."

"He is."

"But you're cute, too. If it ain't him, then you'll find someone else."

"Why, thank you, Piper."

"I'm going to reorganize the garage. If you need me, I'll be out there until about lunchtime, I think."

"I'm going to watch a movie or listen to some music while I run on the treadmill."

"Do you miss the track and field club?"

"I do. We should run together sometime."

"I'd like that. I'm going to get cleaning out in the garage now. Later, sis."

Stevie starts by pulling the buckets of tools over to the pegboard to find them new homes. Then there's a bucket of random nails, screws, and wall anchors that she separates into an organizer drawer. That alone takes hours. Stevie wipes down the planter pots and organizes the potting table near the back door. She uses the big wet/dry vac to gather up the dirt and a long duster for a deep clean on the shelves. Finally, Stevie sprays down the garage from back to front, then waters the flowers that Mom recently potted.

"Piper, I'm done in the garage. I'm going to take a shower and get all this dust off me. Stay inside. Don't answer the door for strangers," Stevie warns.

"Yes, Mom," Piper giggles.

"Funny girl."

Stevie goes down to the basement and vacuums the family room, wipes down the glass and mirror in the tiny workout studio, and jumps in the shower, ending up on her hands and knees scrubbing grout with a toothbrush and wiping down the shower door with the squeegee eight times on each side. By the time she gets to the mirror, it's all steamed up. Stevie swipes it with her hands and looks at herself in the mirror. She bawls until Piper knocks on the door.

When all the other shit was going on, I had less to be OCD about, it seems. Now it's coming at me tenfold and in waves. I can't let Piper see how crazy I am. She might pick up on it and start to do it, even though Shelby says that's not likely.

Stevie picks up her phone after she dries off and gets dressed.

Stevie: Izzy, can we hang out by UR pool?
Nico: Oh, that sounds like fun. Count me in.
Stevie: I've got Piper with me.
Izzy: Mom said yes. It's a go. Time?
Stevie: within the hour?
Izzy: Ya bet.

Nico: Can I invite Elias over?
Stevie: That's up to Izzy.
Izzy: I'm fine with it.
Stevie: Cool.

Epilogue

It turns out I needed the medication change, and I found one with limited side effects of occasional nausea and dizziness, but with maximum benefits in the OCD department. I'm no longer hair-pulling. Plus, I'm sleeping better and straight through the night, which helps with my episodes. Medication and yoga are key. I was doing it all wrong. The focus should be on the breath, not the workout. I'm also running with Piper five days a week. Occasionally, Elias joins us, but he mainly runs with Henry.

As for Elias. We started dating again. I got my driver's license so that I can pick him up now, too. Oh, I got a used car for my sixteenth birthday. Nothing fancy, but it runs well, Dad says.

The OCD group is going great. There are five new people, one of whom Henry is dating. Elias and I sit by them with Zoey on my other side. Sally finally found a friend her own age who really got her talking in the group.

Piper still shows no signs of having OCD. Shelby tells me to stop worrying. Mom and Dad have grown close once again after that week in hell where two funerals, a breakup, and a disclosure almost took me down. But as the adage says, the whole is stronger than its parts. And that's me…going strong with OCD and refusing to let it define me.

Author Note

Mental Illnesses such as Bipolar Disorder and OCD aren't preventable, and unfortunately, most people don't have a fundamental understanding of the mental disorders; therefore, they fear those experiencing the wound no one can see.

We need our society to continue to bring awareness to the mental illness issue that affects forty-six million Americans each year and to place great emphasis on ensuring that those in need have access to proper care and treatment.

If you or anyone you know has been affected by mental illness, you can find help at the organizations below—understand that you're not alone in this struggle. Neither is your family.

National Alliance on Mental Illness
nami.org
1-800-950-NAMI
info@nami.org

National Crisis Text Line
Text HOME to 741741

Active Minds
activeminds.org

The National Suicide Prevention Lifeline
suicidepreventionlifeline.org
1-800-273-8255

Mental Health America
mhanational.org

The Jed Foundation
jedfoundation.org
halfofus.com

Discussion forums and latest news
schizophrenia.com

Anonymous group meetings in your area
saarda.org

S.A.F.E. Alternatives
Selfinjury.com
1-800-DONTCUT

TEEN Lifeline
TeenLifeline.org
1-800-248-8336 (TEEN)

About the Author

Angela Grey is an Indigenous novelist, poet, and painter whose work explores the intersections of memory, identity, and healing. She, formerly an architectural drafter, studied creative writing, as well as spirituality and healing, at the University of Minnesota, where she deepened her commitment to storytelling as both an art and a form of medicine. Alongside her writing, Angela finds balance in yoga and Mindfulness-Based Stress Reduction (MBSR), which shapes the reflective quality of her work. She lives in Eden Prairie, Minnesota, with her husband, one spirited pup, and four cats. When she's not writing, she enjoys camping, budget travel to places like Maine, Oregon, and the coastal Carolinas, and gathering with family around a BBQ grill.

Website: ShadyOakPress.com
Website: angelagrey.com
Tiktok: @authorAngelaGrey
Instagram: angelaellengrey
Facebook: angelaellengrey
Twitter: @AngelaEllenGrey

www.ingramcontent.com/pod-product-compliance
Lightning Source LLC
Chambersburg PA
CBHW070652010826
48975CB00013B/804